LETTING GO

E M Richmond

Dedication

For Jenny, my rock.

For Carol, Mary Ellen, Mary and Steve, who are always there to help me keep my head straight.

And finally to those who also suffer from the 'invisible illness'.

A call in the middle of the night wakes Janet with some bad news. Her best friend has killed herself. Janet looks for answers as she slowly deals with her grief through some journals left behind and discovers her friend has hidden a painful secret.

Her own journey of discovery begins to interfere with her personal life until she almost reaches breaking point. She has help from a man who knew her friend, knew her and cared for her, but never had the chance to tell her. As the pair grow closer, Janet begins to let go, finding hope and love.

This is a story which delves into the consequences of mental illness and suicide. It contains themes of abuse, both physical and emotional, but is ultimately a story of finding the strength to let go. Of hope.

"Every man has his secret sorrows which the world knows not; and often times we call a man cold when he is only sad."

Henry Wadsworth Longfellow

Disclaimer

This book deals with mental illness and depression. It is fictional and in no way represents any one person's individual experience. I would not even pretend to understand how another sufferer would experience the illness – it is unique to them and them alone.

CHAPTER ONE

The harsh bell of the telephone ringing outside my door woke me from a deep sleep. Still groggy, I was tempted to roll over and clap the pillow over my head to muffle the sound until it started to register that it was still dark in the room, which meant it wasn't even close to morning.

Groaning, I rolled onto my side as the ringing became almost insistent, echoing in my ears. I squinted at the numbers on my digital clock, barely able to make them out. Three am, or close enough.

When I was growing up, there had always been a strict rule that no family or friends were allowed to call after nine. Up until I was seven years old, I grew up on a working dairy farm which was now run by my father. Dad was used to retiring around ten o'clock, so he could be up at five the next morning ready for the milking. So if anyone called in the middle of the night, it had to be a dire emergency.

I remembered there was one incident where someone kept calling at two o'clock in the morning; once a week, without fail, for about six weeks. We never knew who it was as the person never spoke, according to my dad. He eventually got onto the phone company and got them to track the calls, but he was so mad.

I kind of enforced that rule with my own friends. I'd had flatmates who had people ringing at all hours and I finally had to put my foot down with them, telling them in no uncertain terms that it better be an emergency or else the phone was getting shut off at night.

So if someone was calling me at three o'clock in the morning, there had to be something wrong.

The phone was still ringing. Only seconds had passed but with my mind still half asleep, it felt like minutes. I stumbled out of bed, tripping over my slippers as I staggered to the bedroom door before opening it and grabbing the phone which stood on a table in the hallway. It was a fixed set and the cord tended to tangle. The sound of the ringing cut out as I picked it up and for a moment I thought I had lost the call.

"Hello?" My voice was still croaky with sleep. I'd always felt like a total dork when it did that as it sounded weird to my ears.

I thought the person had hung up after having waited for so long, as there was no reply on the other end, yet I could hear something. Like snuffling, or little whimpers.

"Hello," I said again, knowing it sounded kind of redundant, but really, I didn't know anyone who could think clearly at that time of morning, especially when they'd been woken up from a deep sleep. I cleared my throat and tried again. "Are you there?"

The sounds increased in frequency and volume. I was going to say 'hello' a third time when a female voice spoke in a hesitant tone.

"Janet?"

I frowned. I thought I knew the voice, but they were sobbing in-between breaths and I couldn't quite tell who they were.

"Yes?" I grimaced. I didn't know why, but it just sounded like a stupid thing to say.

There were more sobs as if she was struggling to get the words out. I held on, trying not to make any impatient sounds.

"It's Callie. She ... she ..."

She what? I thought.

The voice broke and the person on the other end began sobbing as if her heart was broken. I began to get a sick feeling in the pit of my stomach and a cold sweat broke out on my forehead. I took a deep breath, trying to calm myself.

"What happened to Callie?"

"She ... I ..."

I remembered reading about a guy who worked for emergency services in America who told a hysterical girl to stop whining while she was trying to get help for her dying relative. At the time I thought that was quite a rude thing to say, but it had occurred to me that he'd probably been trying to get her to calm down but it had just come out wrong. With that in mind, I knew if I huffed or made any sounds of impatience, it would just make it that much more difficult for the girl on the other end of the phone.

I waited. She was clearly taking deep breaths, trying

to calm herself, but the crying didn't stop.

"What's happened?" I repeated.

"She's … she's dead, Janet."

I'd flown from Wellington, our capital city, to Sydney in Australia for a work conference one year. The flight had been in rough weather and there was a lot of turbulence. There had been one point where I'd almost felt the contents of my stomach come back up to meet me as the plane dropped, hitting a downdraft. That was exactly the way my stomach felt as I heard those words.

"What?" I asked in disbelief.

"I came home and she was … she was … I called the ambulance but by the time they got her to the hospital it was too late."

Now I knew who the caller was. Her flatmate, Susan. They'd been living in the same house for the past few years. I'd met Susan when I'd gone to help Callie move in and we hadn't got along very well. It wasn't that I disliked Susan. I just couldn't understand why Callie would move in with a girl who was everything she wasn't.

It seemed odd that I had been the first person Susan had thought of to call with this news, thinking that maybe she should have called Callie's parents first, but I figured that sometimes people just didn't think rationally when things like this occurred.

Callie was my best friend, and now she was gone. What had happened?

"Susan, have you called her parents?" I asked, trying to figure out her thought processes. It wasn't to say that Susan was unintelligent, but even though we'd had little to do with each other, my opinion of her wasn't exactly favourable.

Susan sounded much calmer as she replied, as if she was over the hardest part.

"I ... I thought it would be better coming from you," she replied.

I nodded, knowing how redundant it was, since she couldn't see me. I supposed she was right. It would be better coming from me.

"You're probably right." I took a deep breath. A million questions had run through my brain and as hard as it was learning the news, there was one more thing I needed to know. "Susan, what happened?"

"She killed herself Janet."

If it had been an accident, or natural causes, I think I could have handled it better. As it was, I nearly dropped the phone in shock. I'd known Callie had a few problems, especially with depression, but the thought that she would do something like this ...

I inhaled and exhaled slowly for a few breaths to calm myself before I spoke again.

"Susan, I need to call Mr and Mrs James. Will you be okay?"

"When can you get here?" she asked, as if it was a given that I would just get in the car and start driving at three in the morning.

"I need to make a couple of calls first, but I should be there about ten-ish."

That gave me roughly six and a half hours to get myself organised and drive from my place to hers. Callie lived ... had lived in Auckland, which was roughly four hundred kilometres away from the

Hawkes' Bay, a small province on the east coast of the North Island of New Zealand. We had never cared about the distance, talking on the phone every few weeks or video calling each other on Skype. We'd been friends nearly all our lives and we'd never let anything change our friendship.

Now everything had changed.

I said goodbye to Susan after making sure she would be all right, then pressed the disconnect button on the phone, preparing to dial the number for Callie's parents.

I couldn't see the buttons on the handset. Rolling my eyes at the inanity of it, I reached over and switched on the light in the hallway, blinking rapidly at the sudden brightness. I began dialling.

I glanced over at the clock on the wall as I waited for the phone on the other end to be picked up. It was three thirty.

"Hello?"

Clearly the phone was right next to the bed as it was picked up fairly quickly. However, the voice on the phone sounded just as addled as I had been when I'd first picked up Susan's call. I wanted to give her a few seconds to adjust but she might have hung up the phone again if I didn't answer.

I was surprised at how calm I was as I spoke to Marion.

"It's Janet. I ... Marion, it's Callie. She ..." I grimaced. How could I tell her mother that her only daughter had killed herself? "She's passed away."

It sounded so ordinary to describe something so terrible, but I couldn't tell her the truth. It was hard enough for me to deal with it.

There was silence on the other end, then a loud clang which hurt like hell as the noise went through my head. I heard Marion speaking to her husband Richard but I couldn't make out what she was saying. She seemed almost unnervingly calm as she spoke.

"I'm sorry," she said. "I dropped the phone. What happened?"

"I'm not sure of all the details. Susan wants me to come up. I don't think she knows what to do."

"Janet, what are you not telling me?"

"I'm so sorry, Marion," I said, feeling the lump in my throat. I could feel the tears threatening but I continued to fight them. She deserved to know the truth, but if I told her I would have to face the stark reality. My best friend had killed herself.

I didn't want this to be real.

CHAPTER TWO

It was Friday, but I had asked for the morning off, so I wasn't due in at work until noon. As soon as I judged it to be a reasonable time, I called my boss to let him know I wouldn't be in for a few days. The sun was just coming up, but Alex had once told me he liked to be up with the birds. He often spent those early mornings taking a walk with his wife, Betty.

"Alex, it's Janet."

"Hey Janet. What's up?"

Alex was not just my boss. He was a friend. I'd worked at the local medical clinic as a physiotherapist for about twelve years, ever since I'd completed my training. Doctor Alex Dawson was not just a GP, he was the clinic's director. He was the kind of doctor who cared about his patients.

He had once had a patient who had been on the waiting list for a year or so for surgery. The patient was not well at all, yet the public hospital kept putting off the surgery. While Alex understood that emergencies took priority, he was not impressed with the hospital's decision that the patient's condition wasn't serious enough for them to give it importance.

Finally, Alex had had enough and sent off a scathing email to the hospital board, denouncing its practices, telling them a person's quality of life was a priority. His patient was in having surgery within a month of that email.

While it was hard to say whether it was the email which forced them to take action or whether it had been already scheduled was difficult to tell, but Alex still took some credit for it. He was known in many of his social circles as the kind of doctor who put his patients' quality of life first and would sooner pay their medical bills himself if it got action.

I hesitated as I thought what to tell him. I'd found a rest area where I could pull off the road and turn off the engine for a few minutes while I called. A few years ago the government banned the use of cellphones while driving, which I thought was a good thing. A friend of mine had lost his sister when a guy who had been on his cellphone while driving had been distracted, crossed the centre line and smashed head-on into her car.

So I was careful to stick to the letter of the law.

"Alex, a friend of mine passed away early this morning."

I heard his shocked gasp.

"Oh my god, Janet! Are you okay?"

It was typical of our friendship that the first thing he would do would be to enquire after my welfare. Alex was about twenty years older than me but he was a caring, compassionate man who put his employees' and his patients' welfare ahead of profit. Yet for all that, no one took advantage of his kindness.

"I'm okay," I told him. It wasn't completely true, but I didn't know what else to say. "I'm on my way up to Auckland now to see her flatmate."

"Well, listen, you take as much time as you need," he told me kindly. "Text me when you know where you're at."

I nodded, even though he couldn't see me.

"Thanks Alex."

I hung up, starting the car again as I put the phone back in my bag. I stared out through the windscreen at the dense bush. I hadn't slept since the phone call and I'd drunk so much coffee I should be buzzing, but I was bone-weary. The kind of exhaustion where I felt like I was awake but nothing was registering and my bones just felt as if they were aching, and so heavy, if I could just close my eyes for a few minutes I would be fine.

I still couldn't believe Callie was gone. So many questions ran through my head. What had happened? Why hadn't she talked to me? Was I a bad friend because I didn't know she was in pain?

The last time I'd talked to Callie had been about a month ago. We'd been talking on and off for a year about going away for a holiday to America. While I wasn't a fan of the place, Callie had always wanted to see Los Angeles. I used to tease her that she only wanted to go to see if she could catch a glimpse of her favourite tv star. She was always getting crushes on Hollywood stars.

"C'mon," I'd said to her when we'd first started talking about the trip. "You just want to go to L.A. so you can meet your boyfriend."

"Shut up," she'd said, blushing. She always blushed when she talked about her crush. "You know, just because you don't get crushes doesn't mean you can make fun of the rest of us losers."

I had frowned at her attitude. Usually Callie had a self-deprecating sense of humour but that had had a more serious overtone to it which nagged at me.

"You're not a loser. Who says that?"

She shrugged.

"People."

"Well, you know what, anyone who says that is the loser. You're amazing, and don't you forget it."

She mock saluted me and laughed.

I sighed, thinking about those conversations. I'd always been able to make her laugh, even when she was down.

A month ago we'd been talking about the trip. Although, when I thought about it, I'd been doing most of the talking and she was just quiet. I should have realised then something was up, but Callie never said anything.

I hit my forehead on the steering wheel.

"You're so stupid!" I told myself. I'd been so caught up in the excitement of making plans for the holiday I'd prattled on and on and never even realised she wasn't saying anything.

God, how selfish could I be?

I put the car in gear and left the rest area, careful to keep my eyes on the road despite my weariness and my distracted thoughts. The last thing I needed was to get in an accident.

The remainder of the drive was quiet, but by the

time I got to the city, the traffic had started to build up. It might be the weekend, but the roads tended to be busy around Auckland.

My first time driving the motorway I was terrified. I'd driven up for a conference as part of my ongoing training and I had found the motorway more than a little daunting. I was used to driving a two-lane highway, not three or four lanes each side. I had no idea what I was supposed to do or where I was supposed to go and I was anxious. I stared straight ahead, my hands so tight on the steering wheel my knuckles turned white.

Callie had laughed at me when I told her. She'd been living in Auckland a couple of years then. She didn't drive and always used the bus or the train. It was pretty much old hat to her, although she once joked the bus drivers must get their training from Formula One drivers with the way they negotiated the city streets.

Auckland was huge. At least by my standards. I was used to a much smaller metropolitan area where the entire population was less than 100,000 people and Auckland had about a third of the country's population squeezed into a less than 2,000 square kilometre area. The central city alone was daunting and every time I drove there I managed to get myself lost.

My mind kept drifting to the last time I talked to her. I hadn't noticed anything different, but ... Had I been so completely full of myself that I really hadn't seen that she was down? Am I really that self-centred? I thought.

I heard a car horn beeping at me and looked up, realising I'd become so distracted that I hadn't noticed I'd drifted into the next lane.

"Come on, Janet, you need to concentrate."

It probably would have been better if I'd got a little more sleep and drank a lot less coffee, given myself time to think, I told myself. Of course, then I would have to think about what had happened.

The truth was, I didn't want to think about it at all. I was still dry-eyed. I should be crying, I told myself. Callie was my best friend. We'd been friends forever.

CHAPTER THREE

The sign for a primary school appeared on my right and it brought back memories of my years at school, and the first time I met Callie.

"Class, this is Janet Kingi. She's going to be with us for the rest of the year."

I was so nervous the first day I faced the Year Two class at Rothman Primary in sunny Napier. We'd just moved to the city from Te Kuiti, which was a small town in the King Country. My dad, Hone, had a beef and dairy farm there, but when he and my mum, Sarah, decided to separate, Mum moved us to Napier. I was so used to living on the farm that being in a sprawling urban centre, not to mention living so close to the coast, was a little overwhelming for me.

The teacher was tall, or at least tall for me, a girl descended from one of the big Maori tribes which much of the lower half of the North Island, although it had scattered over the past few decades. I was small of stature and kind of chubby, with skin which tended to be more olive in the winter and a medium-brown in the summer.

Mrs Henriksen, a kindly-looking blonde in her late twenties, who I later learned was married to a very nice Norwegian man, told me to take my seat, pointing to an empty desk next to a girl who had hair so blonde it was almost white. Her skin was pale enough to be considered translucent and she had a dusting of freckles on her nose.

"You'll look after Janet, won't you, Callie?"

Callie nodded. "Yes ma'am."

She looked at me shyly under pale eyelashes. While she was sitting, I could tell she was much taller than I was. She was pretty. Lanky and slender, not like me with my squat little body, I thought.

Mrs Henriksen started us on maths. I didn't have a maths book, so Callie shared with me. She was good at maths and had the problems solved before I did. She seemed to be a good student who liked school. Unlike me. It was only our second year of primary but where she seemed to fit in, I felt like a fish out of water. Part of it was probably that I'd come from a small school in a small town where the biggest class size was about twenty or so. There were at least thirty children in the class; that I could guess.

We moved on from maths to reading and it was fairly obvious right from the start that Callie was the best in the class. I tried to follow on as best I could but even then it was difficult. Still, Callie was kind enough to help me.

We were sent outside at lunch. The temperature was kind of cool, since it was Autumn, but the teachers thought fresh air and exercise was good for us. So did my dad, really. Besides, I'd spent my first seven years on the farm and that had made me robust, not that I knew what that meant at seven years old.

Callie showed me around the school, including the playground and the hall where we would have to go for assembly. The school was huge in comparison to the little country school I'd been used to. Instead of only about five or six classrooms, there were twenty. I was already lost. The playground had what I liked to call an obstacle course, with concrete tunnels, a rock wall and huge tractor tyres where children were already sitting.

I chattered with my new friend as we walked around before sitting down to eat our lunch. Callie was quiet whereas I was, as my dad used to call me, a chatterbox. Still, she laughed at something I said and made a joke of her own.

Our friendship was pretty much sealed the moment we ate lunch together. We sat down on one of the benches bordering the playground and took our lunchboxes out of our backpacks. I had a themed lunchbox, with a picture of Barbie on the front. I supposed it was my mother's way of trying to discourage me from being a tomboy, but I'd never been a girly girl. Callie's was just a plain plastic container.

Callie sighed and made a face as she opened it up. I looked over and saw she had two sandwiches wrapped in paper and a banana. As she unwrapped it, the displeasure on her face was obvious.

"I don't like jam," she said. "My mum knows I don't like jam."

I looked at my own meagre offering in my lunchbox. I had two peanut butter sandwiches, a yoghurt and a mandarin.

"I've got peanut butter," I said. "Wanna swap?"

Callie lit up in a big smile. "I looove peanut butter!"

Eagerly we swapped sandwiches.

"So how come you moved here?" she asked."

"My mum and dad are getting a divorce."

"What's a divorce?"

"Um, it's where your mum and dad don't live together anymore."

"Oh." She looked crestfallen. "So where are they if they don't live together?"

"I moved here with my mum and my dad still lives on the farm."

Her eyes widened. "Your dad lives on a farm?"

I guessed Callie had never seen a farm before.

The blare of another car horn broke my reverie. I indicated and changed lanes, deciding to get out of the line of traffic. An exit was coming up and I drove on, moving into the exit lane. It would take me a little out of my way before I got to Callie's flat, but I decided it was better than getting distracted and causing an accident on the motorway.

The area where I'd turned off was considered to be some of the poorer parts of Auckland. The houses tended to be shabby; paint peeling off the weatherboard, broken tiles, long, weed-choked grass. As I drove, I saw several front yards with broken toys just lying on the grass as if the children who owned them couldn't care less.

My phone beeped, indicating a text message. I

decided to stop the car and check it, so I could also check my map. I had only been to Callie's place a few times and I still wasn't sure of my directions. I pulled over and parked, ignoring the irritated beep from the driver behind me, then looked at my phone.

Susan had sent me a text asking where I was. I sent her a text back telling her I wasn't far away, then accessed the app for maps. I was at least on the right track, I thought, putting the phone back in my purse and driving off once the way was clear.

Again, I was struck by the appearance of poverty in the area. While it wasn't as bad as some other areas of the city, or the country as a whole, the general demeanour of it was depressing.

Callie grew up in one of the poorer neighbourhoods in Napier. I had probably been a bit naïve in thinking that everyone had money, or owned their own home. Callie's parents weren't like that. She had told me that the place they lived in was rented.

I didn't understand at seven. I don't think Callie did either, really.

"What does that mean?" I asked.

She shrugged. "They pay rent each week to a land lord."

"What's a land lord?" I asked innocently.

Again she shrugged, hunching her shoulders.

"Doesn't your Mum have a job?" I said. I knew her father worked, as a driver for a supermarket chain, although from what she'd told me, it didn't seem he liked his job very much.

She shook her head. "Mum makes the beds and does the dishes and she cooks tea."

My mother had always worked alongside my father on the farm, so the concept of only one parent working was alien to me.

Of course, even then, we didn't see that being a housewife and mother was just as much a job and probably more tasking than her father's job. Still, her mother was part of the generation that believed one parent should always be home with the children. They didn't believe in such a thing as child care.

Callie and I were born at the very end of what a writer once called the 'me decade'. The whole decade had been a period of change for women, at least in other countries. Here in New Zealand, while we weren't that much behind the times, it tended to go unnoticed in the smaller communities.

The poor were still poor and the rich just got richer. My family was lucky, as farming was still a major part of the country's economy. Not that my parents had been rich, I assumed, but in many ways, we were far better off than Callie's family.

Callie always had patches on her clothes where it was obvious her mother had tried her best to repair holes. Or else she would be given clothes from friends in the neighbourhood whose children had already outgrown them. Callie often wore things which didn't suit her. I had hardly been a fashion plate at that age either. Jeans and blouses were pretty much my 'uniform' during the day, until we went to high school.

She didn't talk much about her home life. Her parents were good people, but just didn't seem to know how to improve their situation.

I had once more become lost in my memories and I

missed the turnoff to Callie's street and had to turn around and go back. I finally reached it and indicated my intention to the traffic behind me, waiting for a car to pass before turning right into the street and driving down the hill to the driveway. Callie lived along a tree-lined avenue.

This time of year the trees were losing their leaves and the surrounds were awash with colour. There were two times of year I really loved. Early autumn and early spring. I loved the colours when the leaves were just starting to turn gold, before they fell off the trees, and then when the new shoots were coming through.

Susan must have heard the car as she came out. Even at this distance, I could see that she was a mess. She hadn't brushed her long gingery-blonde hair, which was pulled back into a messy ponytail and her face was puffy as if she had been crying all night. There were mascara streaks on her face, so she clearly hadn't taken off her make-up either.

I braked and turned off the ignition, getting out of the car. Susan barely left me any time to straighten up before she was flinging her arms around me, crying again.

"Janet," she cried.

I managed to grab my bag from the front seat and closed the door walking with her into the house. The door was a little warped and I found it hard to close. I guessed it was from all the rain we'd been having lately. There was a song I loved that I often thought of when I considered New Zealand's climate. It really did feel like 'four seasons in one day' sometimes. Auckland's winters tended to be fairly mild as they didn't get any snow, but autumn could sometimes range from almost summery temperatures to bitterly cold.

I sat Susan down on the couch. The living room was a mess with tissues everywhere. Susan and Callie hadn't exactly been the tidiest of people, but they tried.

"Why don't I make some tea," I suggested gently, prying myself away from her and going to the kitchen to put the kettle on.

Susan was still crying steadily as I waited for the water to boil, yet I was completely dry-eyed. What was wrong with me? My best friend was dead but it was as if I couldn't feel anything.

CHAPTER FOUR

Before I had decided I wanted to be a physiotherapist, I had gone to Waikato University to study for a diploma and I had taken a few papers in psychology. One of the first things I learned was that there are five stages in grief. Denial, anger, bargaining, depression and finally acceptance.

Had I thought about it, I'm sure I would have realised I was in the denial stage. Eventually.

As I went to make the tea, I kept expecting Callie to jump from behind the door and say: 'haha, I fooled you'. Not that she would have. If there was one thing Callie had taken seriously it was death. She had been the one to find her grandfather when he passed away from an aneurysm and it had freaked her out. To her, death was not funny.

It had already been a hard year for Callie when her grandfather died. He'd been admitted to hospital about eighteen months earlier, diagnosed with an aortic aneurysm. Callie's grandmother had been beside herself with fear and anxiety, thinking she was going to lose her beloved husband.

I met them when I was about ten. Callie's grandfather, Bill, was a jovial kind of man who always cracked jokes and teased her like crazy. He was probably the one person, besides me, who could bring her out of her shell. They certainly shared the same sense of humour and Callie's face always lit up in a huge grin when her grandparents visited.

Her grandmother, Mary, was slightly more serious, but she clearly loved her husband, even if she would roll her eyes at his jokes. They were always bickering but never in a nasty way. The banter was something that I think was just a part of their marriage.

Callie once related the story of how her grandparents got together. When they met, Mr and Mrs Shaw hated each other on sight. Or that was how Mary always told it. She used to say that Bill was completely obnoxious and annoyed her from the moment they met. Over time, they began to develop a good friendship, eventually falling in love.

Mary used to say that passion faded, but a marriage that was built on friendship was a marriage that would last. She was right. They were married nearly sixty years.

Mary died about three months before Bill. The day he died, Callie had gone to visit her grandfather. She'd not long moved to Auckland and her grandparents had lived in a modest home in the southernmost end of the city. She had taken the train to visit him, walking down from the station.

She told me when she had got to the house, she had found the door wide open. Thinking someone had tried to burgle the place, she had gone in cautiously and found her grandfather sprawled on the kitchen floor. There was a bag of groceries on the floor next to him. He'd clearly been shopping and had collapsed as he'd got inside.

Callie had never forgotten the incident or how it had felt to find her grandfather like that. So it was a subject she could never joke about.

I finished making the tea and took it out to Callie's flatmate. She had calmed down somewhat, although I could see fresh tears threatening when she looked at me, taking the cup from my hand and sipping the tea. I noticed the cup shaking.

Susan and Callie were complete opposites. While they were both blonde, Susan's hair was brighter. She was more outgoing than Callie; she attracted people to her like bees to honey. It wasn't that Callie was a hard person to get to know. She was just shy. Susan had never had that problem. The thing that used to annoy me about Susan was she was flighty. While she attracted people easily to her, they also tended to come and go easily as well. With Callie, when she made a friend, she made a friend for life.

I tried to ease her into telling me what had happened as gently as I could. For some reason, Susan and Callie had been friends, even though Callie would often complain when Susan was thoughtless. Callie was just the type of person who couldn't say a bad thing about another person.

There was an incident when we were in high school, there had been a group of girls who kept teasing us. It was starting to escalate into bullying. I couldn't take it and wanted to tell one of our teachers, or the principal, but Callie had talked me out of it. The bullying upset her and they seemed to revel in that; it was just typical bully behaviour. Still, she held her head high and tried to say that it didn't matter. Her parents would often tell her to ignore it and it would go away.

My father once tried to comfort me by telling me an old saying: 'Sticks and stones may break my bones, but names will never hurt me'. I happened to think he was wrong. Names and words could and did hurt.

Looking back, knowing what I know now, I wonder if Callie took the bullying because she thought in some screwed up way she deserved it.

Susan's hands were shaking as she told me again how she had come home to find Callie lying on the floor of the bathroom. Because this was a 'sudden death' the hospital had called police and they had found a bottle with a label for prescribed medication on the floor of Callie's room. It had been some kind of anti-anxiety medication which her doctor had prescribed a couple of weeks ago. The bottle was empty.

It occurred to me to wonder if Callie had somehow planned this when she had got the medication or if things had suddenly become too much for her.

What does it matter, you idiot? I berated myself angrily. She's dead. She's dead.

"What the hell happened, Susan?" I asked.

My best friend's flatmate shook her head.

"I don't know. Like I said, I came home and she was … She was still breathing, but only just. I called an ambulance but they said by the time they got her to the hospital she was gone. It was too late to pump her stomach.”

“What time was this?” I asked.

Susan had gone out partying with her friends after work. Callie had gone occasionally but I guessed Susan had decided not to ask her. I just couldn't understand why she would leave her alone in the house if Callie was depressed enough to kill herself.

“You had to have noticed something. Anything.”

“I've been busy with work,” Susan said, sounding defensive.

I wanted to shake her, thinking Susan should have noticed something. It was stupidly irrational. Even I knew through the little psychology I'd studied that people in the depths of depression were sometimes very adept at pretending. If there was one thing I did know about the illness, it was that it wasn't always obvious, even to the most observant of people.

Still, one of the things I had never really liked about Susan was how she could be a little self-centred at times. Maybe Callie was just her flatmate, but they had lived together for at least four years. Was she really so self-centred that she couldn't see that Callie was having problems?

I looked around the room, sighing. While I understood that they weren't allowed to put anything up on the walls, Susan had managed to inject some of her personality into the room, yet I couldn't see anything of Callie's anywhere. The couch had a pretty cover draped over the back and there were small knick-knacks displayed in bookcases. Not even the books were Callie's.

Still, getting angry at Susan wasn't going to change

anything. It wasn't going to bring her back.

I had to make a few phone calls, letting others know what had happened, and that took about an hour. It was almost lunchtime when Susan had to get up to answer a phone call and I got ready to leave, knowing I had a lot to do. Marion had asked me to at least help with arrangements and I prepared myself. I had to call the hospital and talk to the funeral director and get everything organised. Marion was just in no state to do so.

The phone rang again and Susan turned and looked at me, holding out the phone, clearly not knowing what to do.

"Um, it's the police," she said.

"I'll take it," I told her, gently taking the handset from her. "This is Janet Kingi."

"This is Constable Emerson. Are you a relative of the deceased?"

I grimaced, hating the word. Now that Callie was gone, she was reduced to just a thing. She wasn't a person anymore.

"No, but I'm representing her parents. They weren't able to drive up this morning."

"Well, we have preliminary findings. Callie's body has been taken to the morgue."

"Am I able to see her?"

"It's probably not a good idea," the constable advised. I supposed I could understand. They probably would have had to do an autopsy and from what I'd seen on television they didn't exactly leave the body in good shape.

"Okay. What happens from here?"

"Well, it can take a couple of days for all the test results to come through, but I think she'll be able to be released by then."

"Okay. Thanks."

"Uh, I'm very sorry for your loss, Miss Kingi."

I thanked him automatically. It wasn't that he was cold or impersonal. He was just doing his job and I supposed he had faced a few sudden deaths in his time, but it still rankled a little.

CHAPTER FIVE

It took the predicted two days before the morgue would release her body and allow the funeral director to take it for embalming and whatever they had to do before the service, which would be three days later. We had to allow time for any relatives who needed to get time off work.

I stayed in a motel. I just couldn't stay in Callie's room. It seemed kind of morbid. I'd called Alex and told him it would be another few days, telling him exactly why it was taking so long. He was shocked and horrified but told me to take as much time as I needed.

The funeral home wanted to dress her in something and I stopped in at Susan's to pick out an outfit. I had no idea what she liked wearing and it felt a little weird going through her wardrobe. Susan wasn't much help either.

"What about this?" I asked, pulling out a short black dress. It had short sleeves and seemed to be designed to drape loosely over her body, hiding her figure. I couldn't understand that. Callie had always had a nice figure.

When we were twelve, Callie had been embarrassed by the fact she hadn't started to fill out. I tried to tell her that every girl grew at their own pace and while she was a little skinny I didn't think much of it.

"But Amanda's got hers," Callie wailed as we sprawled out on her bed one Saturday afternoon.

"Amanda is about six months older than you."

Callie screwed her face up.

"She told me the other day she got her first bra and she said she felt weird about it 'cause I didn't have one yet."

"I don't either," I told her, but I wasn't as flat-chested as her and it would only be a matter of time before I had to get my own bra.

"You know that bi …" I knew what she was going to say but I shot her a look. Her mother didn't like her swearing and she only did it when she was really upset with someone. Normally she didn't say negative things about people, but if she was extremely upset then she would. It took a lot for her to do so, though.

"Anyway, Dawn kept ragging on me saying stuff like: 'Have you aveloped yet?'. She couldn't even say the word properly!"

Well, not everyone was as smart as Callie, but I agreed. It was dumb. Dawn was the kind of girl who thought everyone should bow down to her and do her bidding. What made matters worse was, she continued to bully Callie to the point where it got physical. The teacher told us her father hit her, but still, I didn't think that was an excuse for her hitting someone.

By the time she was twenty, Callie had developed a

very nice figure. Maybe still a little on the skinny side, but she'd grown into a lovely woman. I just don't think she ever saw that.

I sighed, wishing there had been some way for me to get it through to my friend that she was really better looking than she let herself believe. Still, as they say, hindsight is twenty-twenty and unfortunately it was too late.

Susan looked at the dress, a frown on her face. She looked confused as if she'd never seen the dress before.

"I don't … knoooow!" she said, drawing the last word out in a sort of moan.

I was more than a little irritated with her. I knew she couldn't afford to live in the place on her own. Living in Auckland was so expensive, even in the area they were living in, and you had to be making really good money to afford to rent a place. Buying was just out of the question. Susan had already told me she'd started advertising for another flatmate, the day after Callie had died, and it had struck a nerve.

Callie had been gone two days. Surely this could have waited until things settled down, I thought.

I rummaged through the wardrobe and came up with a summer dress that I didn't quite think was Callie's style. It was long with shoestring straps in a sky blue, decorated with white flowers.

"Ooh, I loved that dress on her," Susan said enthusiastically. "I gave her that dress. She looked so pretty in it, with her hair all curled and …"

Susan went off into some sort of tangent, telling me how she'd forever been trying to get Callie to wear make-up and to see herself in a more positive light. We both sighed, full of regret for what might have been. If only we'd been paying more attention, I thought.

I decided the dress would work and pulled it off the hanger. We'd have to pack up some of Callie's clothes in the next few days. Most of it I imagined would be given to the charity shop; maybe the local Red Cross.

I carefully bundled up the dress and put it in a bag, ready to take to the funeral home. Susan left the room with a sigh and went to make coffee.

Next day Callie's parents arrived at the house. I went to hug them, but they looked away.

Callie got her blonde hair from her mum, but where Marion is slightly darker in skin tone, Callie was fair. Her mother was shorter than Callie by about ten centimetres and they had different builds. Most of that I assumed she got from her father, who inherited the blue eyes and black hair from his Irish ancestry. He was tall at around 175cm, slightly taller than Callie, but not by much.

Marion looked pale but dry-eyed. Richard kept looking everywhere but directly at me as if he couldn't face me. I wondered what that was all about, but didn't call him on it. I was sure he would sooner or later let me know if there was something bothering him.

"Have you picked out a dress?" Marion asked, her voice husky. She clearly hadn't slept well the past few days. Her voice had always been a little deeper than normal but I put that down to her having been a smoker since she was a teenager. She'd given up years ago but it still affected her voice.

I nodded. "The funeral home says we can go see her

this morning."

Marion looked around the flat mournfully as if still trying to come to terms with what had happened. Me, I was still trying to figure out what I was supposed to be feeling. I still hadn't cried. I wasn't sure when or if I could. My mind was full of inane things. All the things I should have said to Callie. All the things we had always promised each other we'd do. Things we never got around to doing and never would.

We left a short time later for the funeral home. The director, the same one I'd spoken to when I'd made all the arrangements, sent me a welcoming and sympathetic smile. I introduced him to Callie's parents.

"Mr and Mrs James, please allow me to express my deepest condolences on your loss."

Marion nodded and thanked the man while Richard again tried to look anywhere but at him. It was as if he didn't want to deal with this. I knew this must be hardest of all on him; he and Callie had been very close.

"Barry," I said in a quiet tone, "we've come to see Callie."

"Of course," he replied. "Please come this way."

I steeled myself, wondering what exactly I was going to be faced with. I'd never seen a dead body in a coffin before. Not that I could remember. When my grandmother on my dad's side had passed away, I was five. We held a tangi which took place over three days. Usually in a tangi, which was a Maori tradition, the coffin was open but my grandmother had died of cancer and her body had just wasted away. My parents had argued about it, my mother saying she didn't want me to be frightened by it.

I was fortunate that my other three grandparents were still living.

I'd chosen a simple coffin for Callie. She'd once joked that when she died she could be put in a cardboard box for all she cared.

"What does it matter? I'm dead anyway," she'd laughed.

It had been a very strange conversation. Still, I'd taken her point and chosen a coffin in pine with brass handles – three on each side. Callie had always loved pine. The pollen from the trees made her sneeze, but she loved the look of the wood. She had once bought a kitset bookshelf in the wood and put it together all by herself, then lovingly stained and varnished it. The bookcase had looked amazing when she'd been done with it. Callie had always been good with her hands. The top shelf had had a big knot in the centre. Callie had once told me that some people didn't like such imperfections, but she thought it gave it character.

The coffin I'd chosen had the same thing. A huge knot right in the centre of the lid. I decided she would have liked that. The wood had been stained and varnished so it gleamed almost a golden brown. The surface of the wood was soft and smooth to the touch as I ran my finger over it, looking down at the body of my friend.

They had made her up to look natural. She was wearing the dress I'd picked out and Susan had been right about one thing. She did look pretty in the dress, with her hair softly curled around her face.

Marion gently caressed her daughter's face, careful not to do anything which might smudge the make-up.

She leaned over and kissed her forehead.

"Goodbye my precious baby," she said softly. She started to cry then, unable to keep back the tears. Richard handed her a handkerchief and she turned away, sobbing.

It was Richard's turn. He stared at his daughter, his face stony. Then he leaned over, doing the same as Marion.

"I'm so sorry," he whispered.

Sorry for what, I wondered. Could it be possible he was blaming himself for what had happened? I watched as he turned away and choked back a sob. The couple held each other, taking comfort in each other's arms.

I stood beside the coffin, looking down at my friend, not quite knowing what to do. An irrational anger surged up inside me. I pictured myself pulling her up, slapping her, trying to make her wake up, stop being so stupid. I wanted to hit her. I wanted to scream at her. Most of all, I just wanted to know why..

CHAPTER SIX

We couldn't hold off the funeral any longer. Almost a week after the phone call which had changed my life, we held the service. The director had asked me what music Callie had liked and I had chosen an album by Sarah MacLachlan. There were a couple of songs which were my friend's particular favourites, even though they were quite sad.

One, especially, had a very sad refrain and a slow beat which to me sounded mournful, but the singer had a beautiful voice that just seemed to echo the pain of the lyrics. I didn't know the background to the songs and I'd tried to look them up online but never found anything. All I knew was that the songs made me want to cry.

It was the first time I'd felt like crying since I'd heard the news. The CD played while people filed into the small chapel at the funeral home. Well, it wasn't really a chapel since we'd opted for a non-secular service. Callie had never been particularly religious.

As I heard the line: *Oh darkness I feel like letting go* I

could hear Callie's voice singing it and it caused a lump in my throat. I must have made a sound as a man sitting behind me touched my shoulder. I glanced at him, but didn't pay much attention, taking comfort in that gentle hand.

It was pouring with rain outside and everyone who came in was either wearing a raincoat or was holding an umbrella. One girl, who couldn't have been older than about fifteen, ran in, her long brown hair dripping. Her clothes were also sopping wet. She'd worn a thin dress in a flowery print that looked a little old for her and she was shivering. She was so skinny it was a wonder she could even stand tall.

Everyone looked around at her and I could see her cheeks reddening in embarrassment. I got up and quietly asked Barry, who would be conducting the service, if he had a towel for the girl and he nodded, approaching an assistant, or whatever they were, whispering something in their ear. The younger man went off, coming back a couple of minutes later with a soft, fluffy bath towel, handing it to me. I took it to the girl and she smiled at me gratefully.

"I'm sorry," she said. "I don't have an umbrella."

"It's all right. Let's just get you dried off." She was still shivering but hopefully we could get her dry enough so she'd be a little warmer.

"I'm Miranda," she whispered.

"Janet."

She smiled softly. "Callie told me about you. You're her best friend."

I nodded. "Come on," I said. "We're about to start."

She sat next to me, doing the best she could with the

towel, still looking a little embarrassed, but at least happier.

I glanced around the room. I estimated only about twenty people had come, but they all seemed to have reason to be there.

The service got under way. We'd deliberately picked something short, with readings of poetry rather than prayers. Callie had told me a couple of years ago how she had gone to a Catholic service for her great-aunt, who was very religious. The funeral Mass had been held in a huge church, although not even a hundred people had gone. Apparently the aunt hadn't been very well-liked in the family. According to Callie, she was known as something of a battleaxe.

Callie had laughed when I had rolled my eyes. We'd been talking about the funeral on Skype.

"So, there I am, sitting on this horrid wooden bench ..."

"I think they call that a pew," I told her.

"Whatever! Anyway, I had to sit there for two hours! Oh my god, it was so uncomfortable. You should have heard my cousin Joe though. He was sitting in the row in front of me with his Mum and Dad and the first time the priest said 'let us pray' he went 'oh no'. The second time it was 'not again'. The third time he sort of let out this really loud groan and practically everyone in the church heard it. He was not popular," she laughed.

"When I die," she continued, "don't you dare do that to my family."

Looking back, I sometimes wondered if she knew she would die young.

Barry finally fell silent and asked if anyone would like to get up and say a few words about the deceased. I felt an odd lurch in my stomach. I hated that word. Why did it have to be so impersonal?

I understood on some level. He didn't know Callie. He didn't know she was a bright, wonderful person who gave so much of herself but expected nothing back.

To my surprise, Miranda got up and approached Barry, who stood just above the coffin. Miranda took the microphone from him and turned to look at the crowd.

"I met Callie a year ago. Me and my Mum were living on the streets, 'cause Mum couldn't get a job. Mum was sick, you see, but we couldn't get the benefit 'cause then they would make her go to work and she couldn't do that and I couldn't even get a job at the mall, 'cause they said I was too young. Mum had to leave my Dad because he used to beat her, and then she got sick and she was afraid they would take me away from her. Anyway, Callie helped us out with food and stuff and gave us some of her wages so we could get a room at a shelter.

"My Mum's still sick and now she's in the hospice and Callie found me a place to stay with a friend of hers and she was always helping me out with food, even though she didn't have much money for food either. Now I have a job, even though I'm s'posed to go to school and stuff, but I told them I was older and I'd left school already. It's good work even though I don't like it much, but Callie helped me get the job and I'm sorry she's gone. I wish I could have helped her," she finished sadly.

That was so Callie, I thought. Always taking in strays. She just couldn't stand by and watch someone else suffer.

When she was about nine, she found a kitten wandering around the streets. It looked so young, not even old enough to leave its mother. She argued with her father, hoping he would let her keep it.

"But Dad, it's just a little kitten. Why can't we keep it?"

"We can't afford a cat," he told her sternly, adding that he would contact the local SPCA and get them to take it.

She called him heartless and tried to sneak the kitten to her room, but he caught her.

Miranda's story was so typical of a lot of people. A lot of women left abusive relationships, ending up living in shelters. While there was support, some of them were afraid to ask for that help thinking that they would be required to jump through too many hoops. It sounded to me like Miranda's mother was terminally ill and it was more than likely what had finally prompted her to leave her partner, or husband, whatever he was.

A few more people got up to say something, but Callie's parents stayed silent in their seats, grief etched on their faces. They hadn't had the easiest relationship with their daughter, from what I'd seen over the years. I guess they didn't know how to deal with Callie's illness.

I finally got up.

"Callie was my best friend. We've known each other

since primary school. The thing is, we couldn't have been more unlike each other if we tried, but I think that was part of it. I'd just moved from the farm to Napier and I didn't know anybody but the teacher made Callie show me around. We swapped sandwiches at lunchtime and from then on we were friends.

"I was kind of loud and boisterous while she was quiet and gentle, but that's one of the things I loved about her."

I laughed. "I remember once during the school holidays … I think we were about fourteen or fifteen and I went to stay with my dad on the farm. Well, I asked Dad if Callie could come and stay for a week. The first couple of days we were so excited to be together we talked all night. Dad used to say he couldn't shut us up. But that was Callie. She could be reserved around strangers but once she got to know you, she could talk your ear off. She was the kindest, most compassionate person I've ever known and I loved her like a sister."

I pressed a finger to my lips, then touched the head of her coffin.

"Sleep well, dear sister. I'll miss you."

As I went back to my seat, I felt the dam burst. I started crying, the tears falling down my face. I cried so hard I didn't think I would be able to stop.

CHAPTER SEVEN

We all gathered outside in the rain as the coffin was taken out to the hearse. Callie's wish was to be cremated. I had wanted to object, but had to recognise that we came from two different cultures. To Maori, the human body is sacred, which is why we prefer burial, but this was Callie's preference. She had often remarked that she was squeamish when it came things like decomposition, and had never been able to tolerate that kind of thing on forensic type television dramas. I tried to tell her that it wouldn't matter if she was dead, but we still went with her wishes anyway. Her ashes would be given to her parents to decide what to do with them.

With the completion of the service, we all gathered in the small hall next door which the funeral home had for what we would call a post-tangi feast. I always thought it was called a wake for other cultures, but maybe not. Some would say it was meant to be a celebration of the person's life, but I didn't feel like celebrating. Mostly people came just for the food. And to comfort each other, I supposed.

I took a little time to compose myself, washing my face in the bathroom before going out to face the people. I did a quick count and my earlier estimation was right. Twenty people had come. I didn't know all the faces, but every one of them seemed to have a little story of how they'd met Callie. Some of them had been like Miranda. Strays Callie had 'adopted'.

I often wondered about funeral services. I heard all the time about how, when some well-known person dies, hundreds of people would go to the service, but it always occurred to me to wonder: did they really know the person or were they just going to make sure the person was really gone? It sounded harsh, I knew, but why go to the funeral for someone you barely pay lip-service to?

Maybe only twenty people came to Callie's, aside from her parents, me and her flatmate, but these were people she had touched in some way.

Callie once joined a social networking site on the internet and had over a hundred 'friends'. When I'd asked her about it, she had told me that she knew most of them only through various acquaintances, but wouldn't have known them if she met them in the street. It was the same with a lot of people, I thought. I had my own account too, but I had only a few friends who I could really count as friends.

How many of Callie's 'friends' on that site, I wondered, would have been there for her in a crisis? Seeing how many actually came to say goodbye, I think that answered that.

The caterer for the funeral home had provided finger

food and coffee. I wasn't hungry. I just couldn't see the reason for it. They were eating and supposedly 'celebrating' the life of my best friend. What was there to celebrate?

I decided to get a coffee and picked up a cup, pouring the coffee from the huge urn, adding soy milk and three teaspoonfuls of sugar. I remembered the first time Callie saw how much sugar I liked in my coffee.

"You want coffee with your sugar?" she'd teased.

For a moment I smiled, remembering her sweet voice. She had always teased me about my sweet tooth.

"You'll get fat," she'd say, still laughing at me.

When we met I was this short, dumpy Maori girl while she was tall and skinny. We couldn't have been more disparate if we tried. She would constantly tease me about my stature, but I would give it right back to her. That was just the way we were. We were never mean-spirted about it though.

I'd lost a lot of the chubbiness since then. I'm not skinny, but I'm not overweight either. I'm comfortable with who I am.

Callie never was. She could laugh and tease me about things like my sweet tooth, but she could never accept herself. That was what hurt the most.

"That's a lot of sugar," a deep voice commented beside me.

"Yeah, I have a sweet tooth," I said, turning to look at the man. I recognised him as the man who had sat behind me in the service. He was about my age, or in his late thirties, good-looking, with black hair in a short spiky sort of style. His bright blue eyes seemed to bore through me.

He was an incredibly attractive man, with a smooth, handsome face which could have easily graced the cover of a men's magazine, like GQ or something.

"I'm Tom," he said. "I work … worked with Callie. We were good friends."

"Janet," I said, reaching out and shaking his hand.

He smiled. "Callie mentioned you a few times."

"All good I hope," I said, trying to lighten the moment.

"Oh yeah. She had a lot of good things to say about you." He sighed softly. "You know, it was a huge shock to all of us when we heard. We all thought Callie was a very bright, very special woman. A lot of us did sort of wonder why someone as bright as her was in such a dead-end job. She could have been so much more."

He turned back to the table and poured himself a glass of orange juice.

"We used to talk during our lunch breaks. I knew she was unhappy with what she was doing, but she didn't know any way out. I guess sometimes people just get stuck, thinking that's all they're worth."

I understood. People had put Callie down all her life and while she never said, I knew she thought that that was how it was always going to be. That maybe deep down she deserved the put-downs.

She had worked as an administration assistant, but it bored her. She preferred being in the outdoors. She once said she wanted to be a builder, or do something working with her hands.

Maybe if she hadn't been persuaded to get an office job when she left school, she might have got an apprenticeship as a cabinet-maker. She had always been good with something like that. Trouble was, her dad was kind of an old-school thinker who believed that women should work in office jobs and didn't work in such professions. Callie once joked to him that his attitude went out with the dinosaurs and he gave her such a look that she never brought up the subject again.

When Callie wasn't bogged down in depression, she was fun to be around. We both had the same weird sense of humour. There had been many times at school where we were sent out of class for giggling too much and told not to come back until we'd calmed down.

We had so much in common. We both loved to read and make up stories and we loved to read and act out plays. Our teacher would often pick out plays in the School Journal and we eagerly put our hands up for parts. I think in many ways, acting let Callie be free in ways she couldn't be at home.

It wasn't that her parents were bad. They loved her. Sometimes, though, I got the impression she felt a bit suffocated. Her parents didn't want her doing anything that might get her into trouble. Not that she would. I'd often heard others in the class talking about how she was such a teacher's pet, or she was a goody-two-shoes. I usually threatened to beat up anyone who said that about her. Callie just liked to keep her head down.

When we got older, I went off to begin studies for my chosen career while Callie had worked in a few minimum wage jobs, then found a job working in an office. She wasn't happy in the job and left after a few months. She was desperate to go to university too, but her parents were poor and they couldn't afford to send her. She could have borrowed money, I suppose, but they didn't want her getting into debt either.

I supposed that was when things started to get really bad for her. She felt like a loser. While I became a physiotherapist, and had a job I loved, Callie's life just seemed to get worse. She struggled to find something which made her happy. I'd always wished there was something I could do to help her, but whenever I asked her about it, she would tell me everything was fine.

Tom sighed and shook his head, taking a sip of his orange juice. He squared his shoulders. I wondered if they'd been more than friends. He wasn't saying it verbally, but his body language suggested he cared about her a lot.

He turned and looked at me, seeming a little disconcerted by the way I was studying him. I'd always had a bad habit of staring at people. It was mostly unconscious, and I only became aware of it when they started to show signs of feeling a little uncomfortable, looking away from me, or fidgeting.

Tom wasn't doing any of those things, but to my surprise he was blushing. I wondered if he was shy or something.

"Uh, anyway," he said, putting a hand in the inner pocket of his suit jacket and taking a small card out. "If you ever want to talk, I've been told I'm a good listener."

"Thanks. I appreciate that."

People began to leave and Callie's parents

murmured they wanted to go too. I helped them clean up and we left the hall together. Susan was standing by her car, looking anxious, and I approached her.

"You okay?" I asked as I hugged her.

She nodded, then shook her head, looking as if she wanted to cry again.

"I, uh, I found something. In Callie's room. I thought she'd like you to have it."

Mr and Mrs James hadn't got around to packing up all of Callie's things. I thought they just couldn't face that their daughter was gone. Like if they packed everything up then it would make everything more real.

I hadn't seen a lot of death. My parents are both still alive, although my Mum has since remarried. I called them the day I heard about Callie's death and they were both equally shocked. They had loved Callie almost as much as I did.

I followed Susan in my car back to the flat. I had to get back home, as I'd taken a few days' unpaid leave for the funeral, and I was due back at work tomorrow. It might sound a bit harsh, but life does have to go on, unfortunately.

Still, it had all been kind of surreal. It feels like when the news comes that a loved one has passed away, it's like existing in a kind of bubble. It was like that for me in a lot of ways. I kept wondering why people were still going about their lives when for me it was like the world had stopped turning. Almost like I had expected them to be as touched by the loss as I was.

Realistically, I guessed I was still in denial. I kept expecting her to call me and tell me it was all a mistake, or a dream. That it happened to somebody else.

I dreamed about her, the night before the funeral. She was in a white dress; she hated wearing white because of her blonde hair and white skin. It just made her look washed out. She once threatened to dye her hair jet black, which probably would have looked great with her skin colour, but her parents looked absolutely horrified. They were both blonde haired and blue-eyed and had never even considered changing. Or so they said.

In the dream, she looked, well, to use a cliché, angelic. Of course, I'd heard it said that in some religions, it's believed when a person commits suicide, it's an automatic entry to Hell. I didn't know what to think about that. I wasn't sure I believed in God or heaven, even though I had vague memories of going to church when I was little. As far as I was concerned they were wrong.

I wanted to believe that wherever my friend is, she's happy.

Callie's parents didn't want to come back to the house with me. Once we got to the flat, Susan handed me a cardboard box. I glanced at the contents and saw it was filled with at least fifty hard-backed red notebooks. Callie had a computer but she always liked to write things down in notebooks, although she had never told me what was actually in the books. I picked up one of them and realised they were journals. Callie had recorded everything.

Susan was right, I thought. Callie would have wanted me to have them, since I was probably the one person who did know the depth of her pain. I doubted even her parents really understood it.

Here was where I would find my answers, I thought.

I didn't want to say that I was angry at Callie, but part of me was and I couldn't deny that. Even in the midst of trying to organise everything, I kept asking why. Why had she done it? Why couldn't she come to me?

Callie was proud, I knew that much. She'd been brought up to believe that you didn't ask for help, even from those you loved. Her father was like that. A proud man, Richard thought asking for help was a weakness. I wasn't sure if he'd ever really accepted that Callie was ill. When she had first told me about her illness, she said she had told her parents, but her father had acted so dismissive she hadn't brought up the subject again.

That was the thing about depression. I remembered reading that it could sometimes be an invisible illness. I couldn't remember who said it but there was a quote which went something like: 'everyone has secret sorrows the world knows not'.

Callie had managed to hide it very well, at least, from most people. She had always been good at acting. I wished I could say for sure she never fooled me but the truth was, I didn't know. We didn't drift apart or anything, but living in different cities, leading different lives, I guessed sometimes it happened that we could miss the little things.

Still, Callie could have come to me, I thought. I would have gladly helped her. It just hurt that she didn't feel she could talk to me. We'd been each other's sounding board for years. She'd listened to my boyfriend troubles and to my crazy ideas, giving me the proverbial whack upside the head when she thought I was getting out of my depth and I would do the same to her.

When I was about twenty, I got involved with a guy who I later found out was into the drug scene. I was not a goody-two-shoes by any means but that was the kind of scene I preferred to stay well away from. Still, I had really liked the guy and I confessed all to Callie when I had gone to visit her.

"You're an idiot," she said, giving me a weak punch in the shoulder.

"No, I'm not. I just like him."

"Then he's an idiot. Obviously he can't appreciate you for the amazing person you are if he's doing something you don't agree with."

"I know," I said, drawing it out like a sigh. "I'm just too amazing."

"Hah, the ego on you."

"Look who's talking!" I returned.

"Oh whatever!" she retorted with a huge grin.

There was another time when she'd been having trouble at work. She had been working in the local supermarket, while I was still studying. There had been a guy who kept harassing her, trying to get her to go out with him, but she didn't like him and definitely did not want to go out with him. When she finally told him to get lost, he spread a story around the store that she was a 'tease' and, much worse, accusing her of theft. Her boss had called in her asking for an explanation, threatening to fire her. He just wouldn't listen to her side of the story.

She'd called me in tears and I'd immediately driven to her place to see her. I'd advised her to look for another job, then tried to bolster her spirits with the most trite clichés I could come up.

"You know, it's always darkest before the dawn. You've just got to stay positive. Always look on the bright side of ..."

"Oh shut up!" she said, rolling her eyes and poking her tongue out at me. She laughed and I knew then she would be okay.

Making each other laugh. That was how we'd roll with the punches.

Now though, I would never hear her laugh again, because she was gone. It hurt. Like a pain deep within. She was my dearest, oldest friend and we loved each other.

CHAPTER EIGHT

It was dark by the time I got home and I had to be up at six the next morning to go to work. I picked the box up and took it inside, locking my car, laying it gently on the coffee table. As much as I wanted to go through the books, there was no way I could get to it tonight. It had been an exhausting and overly-emotional few days and I was too tired to think, let alone read.

I woke up late the next morning, the sun pouring in the curved windows.

I live near the beach, in a house that's about eighty years old. It's like a lot of houses in the city that were built after the earthquake of 1931. The city was pretty much flattened in the 'quake. A lot of people died after buildings collapsed. When they were rebuilding, they brought in engineers who studied why the collapses occurred and made sure those defects would be fixed. Napier is on a faultline, but so are a lot of other places in New Zealand. It was just the first really bad earthquake that had resulted in a major loss of lives.

The architecture around the time, which they called

art deco, was supposedly popular after World War I. When I first bought the house, I did a little research on the style, not that I really understood that much what I was reading. I bought it for practicality rather than aesthetics, as it was close to work and it was within my price range. The only thing that kind of bothers me is it's pretty much uniform with the rest of the houses in the street, with curved exterior walls rather than angular. At the time, I suppose it was considered modern, but now it seems kind of kitsch.

The one thing I do like is getting the sun streaming in every morning. When it's not raining that is. Except certain times of the year when the sun pouring in means I'm late for work. I scrambled out of bed, wondering why the alarm hadn't woken me up and glanced at the clock radio on the bedside stand. The volume had been turned down, and as a result I had missed the alarm. My boss wouldn't give me a hard time about it, but I'm one of those people who really don't like being late for anything.

I showered quickly and toasted some bread, spreading jam on it. I was hit with the memory again of that first lunch Callie and I had shared. She still didn't … hadn't liked jam.

The box was still sitting on the coffee table where I had left it the night before. It seemed to be staring at me, reminding me a little of my favourite book when I was a child. I really did feel like Alice, who would be faced with something saying 'eat me' or 'drink me', except the contents of the box were saying 'read me'.

I was already late for work and I had promised Alex I would be in. My boss was understanding but he would worry.

"Sorry, Callie," I said quietly. "I promise when I get home tonight."

With a sigh, I checked the clock and picked up my keys, rushing out the door.

My friends at work were sympathetic, giving me hugs and telling me if I needed to talk they would be there for me. I managed to get through a day's work without wanting to break down. Work at least helped take my mind off things.

I loved my job as a physiotherapist. It could be hard work at times, but it made me feel like I was doing some good. A big plus was the great working environment. Alex had made a point of taking on people who loved what they did and were outgoing and friendly. I liked my colleagues at the medical centre. They were a great bunch of people to work with who genuinely cared about others.

I returned home intending to cook myself some dinner then sort through the box, which I hadn't moved, but you know what they say about good intentions.

My phone was ringing as I put down my keys. I picked up the cordless and pressed the 'Talk' button.

"Hey Chook!"

My dad had always called me Chook. I think it stemmed from when I was little. Dad and I used to tease each other. We had the same laugh, and as my mother would say, be silly buggers. We were both ticklish, and there was nothing my father loved more when I was a child than sitting on the floor with me playing tickle games. It was silly, but I loved it. Mum would call us both silly chooks and that was where the nickname came from.

"Hi Dad."

"How are you doing, sweetie?"

It was just a casual enquiry, but there was an underlying note of concern in his voice. I had a great relationship with my father. There had been times when I was a child, after my parents' divorce, that I had wondered whether he might be trying too hard to make up for what had happened.

I used to wonder why they really got a divorce as they seemed to be good friends. My father sat me down once and explained that sometimes people realised they were better off being friends than being married, and that was what had happened between him and my mother. Sure, money being tight had been a big part of it too, he'd told me, but the reality of it was their marriage just wasn't working.

There had been a couple of kids in high school whose parents had also split up, but those splits hadn't been at all amicable. I heard that with one of the couples, the husband had cheated numerous times. I'd asked my father if he'd ever done that but he had told me that no matter how bad things were, cheating was wrong. I wouldn't say my father was a too good to be true kind of man, but he had strong morals.

The good thing about my parents' relationship post-divorce was that they never had a bad word to say about each other. I never knew whether that was because of me or because they genuinely still cared about each other. All I knew was that I had two parents who cared enough about each other and about me to not go down that road, and I was grateful.

My father chose not to get married again, but a couple of years ago he began seeing a woman in town. I'd met her a couple of times and she was nice. She'd never been married herself but that didn't worry my dad. They had a good time together and it made his life a little less lonely.

I worried about him as much as he worried about me. I'd called him from Auckland the day I'd driven up there to tell him what had happened. Even in his shock, he was concerned at the fact that I'd driven up to the 'big smoke' as he liked to call it. I wouldn't say my father was parochial, but he had never liked the big city. He was very much a country man at heart.

"I'm okay," I assured him. "I got home late last night."

I'd sent him a text as soon as I made it home just to tell him I was home and safe.

"Yeah, I got your message. I'm glad you made it home safely. You know I hate you driving on that road up north."

I suppressed the urge to roll my eyes. Dad meant well, but like I said, he's not a fan of the city. He often checks the paper for any news of accidents on the highway and uses the articles to remind me just how unsafe it was out there.

"That road, Dad, is called a motorway, and it's fine if you know what you're doing and ..."

"Keep an eye on the rest of the idiots," he finished. "How was the service?"

"It was okay. Nothing too fancy, just like Callie would have wanted."

"So how are you really doing?"

I sighed as I sat down on the couch and took off my shoes.

"Really, Dad? I don't know. I'm still having a hard time believing what's happened. I just ... I wish I knew why she did it."

"Oh honey, I know. You and Callie, you were like two peas in a pod."

"No, we weren't," I tried to argue, laughing at him. "We couldn't have been more unlike each other if we tried. But I kind of get what you're trying to say, Dad. I loved her like a sister, and she felt the same way."

He sighed. "I remember when you were teenagers and she came to stay for a week. I think you were about fifteen or sixteen. You two giggled all night. I never got any sleep that week."

I remembered that, since I'd spoken about it at the service. My father's tone made it sound like he was put upon but I knew he didn't mean it. He had loved having her for the week. He had been a little concerned at her shyness but soon had her chattering away to him like they were old friends.

We talked a little more and reminisced about all the good times Callie and I had had together. The memories were comforting, like an old worn out blanket wrapped around me and it felt good to just talk. I rang off with a smile on my face and began making dinner.

An hour later, I finally had a chance to sit down and sort through the books. I was stunned to realise that Callie had been making a journal right from the age of eight. There was a journal for each year of her life.

Sometimes she would write something every day and sometimes she wouldn't write for days, but then she would write a couple of pages.

Finding the first journal, I sat down to read. The entries were written in a childish hand. Most of it was about the little things we did together. From those early entries I could tell she loved having a best friend. Callie's shyness had been a bit of a stumbling block in those early years, but as I read, I could tell she was coming out of her shell a lot more.

She wrote well, injecting a lot of humour into those early years. Most of it was an absolute pleasure to read. There were times when I got the sense she didn't understand why her life was the way it was. I read hints here and there of the illness that she would be diagnosed with years later.

There was one that worried me a little.

I get mad at Janet sometimes. I mean, she talks a lot about life on the farm and I get so mad because it sounds so great, not like with my mum and dad. I know her mum and dad are divorced, and I looked that up so I know what it means now. It means they don't want to be married anymore and they went to see a judge who let them not live together.

My mum and dad fight sometimes. I hear them sometimes when they think I'm asleep. It's mostly about money. Dad doesn't want to get another job even though he hates his job. I don't know why he hates it. I think it's cool. I like going out on deliveries with him because the ladies give me lollies. Or fudge. I like fudge.

I bet Janet thinks it's kind of funny that we live in a house we don't own. A lot of kids my age would think it's weird to live in a house that the government owns. I just know that I hate it because it means we're poor. Only the poor live in government houses. Only the poor have clothes that their mum gets from other people, or from the second hand shops.

I hate being poor.

It hurt to read. I had never thought of Callie as weird for living in a state-owned house. I knew enough to know that not everyone could afford to own their own house. My mother, before she remarried, had also lived in a house she rented. My father owned the farm, but it was mortgaged up to the hilt and while I didn't know a lot about it at eight, I knew there had been financial problems. The two years before my parents decided to split up the farm had had some lean times.

Of course, I hadn't known all the reasons at the time, but even at seven years old, I knew life wasn't a fairy tale and sometimes bad things happened. I wasn't naïve, but I did get the sense that Callie was in a lot of ways. I think her parents tended to be over-protective. I wondered if things would have been better if her parents had actually been more open with her about their financial problems. I sensed a lot of resentment for her situation because she didn't really understand why things were the way they were.

What I realised from reading the journal was that Callie seemed to be comparing herself to me and I had never really paid attention enough to be able to tell her that my life wasn't as perfect as she had thought it was. Maybe that sounds like I blame myself for her problems, but I think we do that when something like this happens. We wonder if there's something more we could have done, or something we could have done differently.

It's funny, really, how we seem to get a distorted view of other people's lives, yet we don't always see our own blessings. I always used to envy Callie because her parents were still together, even though I did come to the realisation that my parents had not been happy together. It hadn't been anyone's fault, really. As I had once explained to Callie, sometimes people change.

In my view, Callie had a nice home, which her mother took pride in keeping clean and tidy and it was always a great place to go to after school. Marion was always baking and there were often delicious smells awaiting us when we arrived at Callie's place. I didn't care that they didn't own the house they were in. It never even occurred to me to think that Callie was a 'loser' as she seemed to feel. It all comes down to how you see yourself, I suppose.

The house they rented was nothing like the home I have now. It was more modern, having been built in the late sixties, a single-storey brick ranch style house, with a slanted tile roof. It was always warm and cosy in winter and cool in summer.

Her parents no longer have that house, although they still rent. They had to move into a two-bedroom home when Callie moved out. Her father left his job a few years ago and now Marion works as an administrator. The money's better, enough, at least, for them to afford a slightly better place, but from what I can tell they still have a few money problems.

My own childhood home, by comparison, was sometimes a lonely place. My mother had moved to

Napier as she had managed to get a job, working for the city council. She worked long hours and often came home exhausted. When I was younger, she would ask the neighbour to look after me for a couple of hours, until she came home. When I made friends with Callie, I was often spending those hours at her house.

Mum didn't appear to mind, thinking it was easier. At least she knew where I was.

I continued to read Callie's first journal that night, alternately laughing and crying at the entries. She related how one afternoon we'd been rehearsing for a school play which we'd have to do in class. I can't remember the exact story, but I think we were pretending to be gangsters.

Neither one of us had seen the movie The Godfather, but we knew enough about it that we could imitate Marlon Brando, to a degree. This particular afternoon, we'd been sitting on Callie's bed, going through our lines and of course, one of the lines was very similar to one from the movie.

Callie got up and started horsing around, walking around the room with a swagger as she pretended to be this tough guy. Then she tilted her chin, scratching at it with her fingers and spoke in a hoarse voice:

"I'm going to make him an offer he can't refuse." It wasn't a perfect imitation of Brando by any means, but I thought it was hilarious, practically rolling around on the bed giggling madly.

Callie looked at me as if I was an alien suddenly come down from some weird planet. I could tell she was trying to look totally serious but her lips were twitching.

I forget how the rest of the afternoon went or even how the play went, but that afternoon we laughed until the tears were practically streaming down our faces. Callie had her serious moments, but she had the most wonderfully wacky sense of humour.

I finished the journal thinking about all those times we had together as children, wishing that I could somehow go back in time and get those moments back.

As I closed the book, I glanced at the clock. It was almost eleven and I'd been reading for about four hours. I was tired, exhausted really, but I didn't want to go to bed just yet.

The phone rang, a harsh sound in the stillness. I frowned at it, wondering who would be calling, not recognising the number on the screen. I had signed up for Caller ID when I hooked up the phone in my place, although the night Susan had called about Callie, I had barely been awake enough to even look at the screen.

The number was an Auckland number, but I knew it wasn't Susan. I wouldn't like to say we parted on bad terms, but I don't think either of us were in any kind of state to be friendly.

I didn't think it would be a telemarketer, since most companies didn't have people working this time of night, unless it was one of those overseas companies which called claiming my computer had a virus and would try to scam me out of hundreds of dollars. One, I'm not that stupid and two, I rarely use my computer, unless it's for work or talking to someone on Skype. I laughingly call myself a techno-dummy. Me and computers just do not click.

"Hello?" I said warily.

"Janet?"

I frowned at the unfamiliar male voice.

"Yes?"

"It's Tom. I got your number from Susan."

Tom? I thought quickly, then remembered. The good-looking man from the service.

"Oh, hi."

"Uh, how are you?" he said hesitantly. "I'm glad you got home okay."

I sat down, relaxing. Tom had a nice voice with a pleasant deep timbre.

"I'm okay. Well, as good as can be, I suppose. Yes, I got home pretty late last night."

"It was kind of surreal at work today. Some of our colleagues didn't go to the funeral but there was this one girl ... she came to me and started crying, yet I knew from a friend that she barely even knew Callie. From what I heard, they barely even tolerated each other."

"Well, maybe I'm reaching, but sometimes people, when they get a shock like that, it makes them take a long, hard look at themselves."

"I guess. I miss her," he sighed.

I heard the regret in his voice and I remembered my earlier thought. That perhaps he had wanted something more than friendship.

"Tom, were you and Callie, uh, more than friends?"

It sounded so awkward and I was taken aback by the silence that followed. I heard a sound almost like choking and I wondered if he was trying not to cry.

"I wanted to, but I never got up the courage to ask her out. I don't know if she would have ever gone though. I mean, she never saw herself as anything special, but I thought she was beautiful."

"She was," I agreed.

"I tried telling her that, but I don't think she ever believed me."

"Callie ... she heard a lot of negative stuff when she was growing up and I guess it kind of stuck."

"That's so sad," he said. "I mean, I've gone out with girls who really only see me for my looks and they don't care about what's underneath, but I could tell Callie really did care about that. That's what made her so special. To me anyway."

Tom seemed to me to be kind of shy. I know that sounds odd, especially when he happens to be a man, and gorgeous as well.

"Well, look, I'm sorry to call so late. You probably have work tomorrow. I just wanted to call and see how you were doing."

I got the feeling that he needed to talk to someone who had been close to Callie. Someone who understood his own pain.

"I appreciate that Tom," I said.

I doubted he would call again, but some small part of me hoped he would. Of course, there was nothing stopping me from calling him either. Our contact had been brief, but I couldn't help thinking there was something very special about this man.

CHAPTER NINE

My work began to suffer as I was staying up late reading Callie's journals. I knew my boss and my clients noticed; how could they not? I was tired all the time, but I couldn't stop reading. I knew the answer to why she killed herself was in there somewhere, but while there were hints of what she had been going through, there was nothing that really stood out as the catalyst.

Part of me thought that perhaps there hadn't been any one incident that had caused it and instead a number of things that had added up over time. I'd read of it happening. But I'd always thought Callie was a strong person, in spite of her illness. Not that I felt she was weak for doing what she did.

I'd once read about someone who had suffered from similar problems. The person had talked about how many times they had almost given up, but something had always stopped them from giving up completely. I just couldn't believe that the girl who had been my best friend nearly all my life could just give up.

So I kept reading, hoping she'd tell me.

Most of the time, what I read gave me the impression that she really didn't see herself the way others did. I remembered reading a couple of lines from a poem – Robert Burns, I thought. The poem had a line about having the power to see ourselves as others see us. In many ways I supposed we tended to get a distorted view of ourselves, especially when we were self-conscious of a particular flaw or lacking in confidence. After reading that poem I thought it would change a lot of things if we did have that power.

I had never been very good at poetry or English lit, as a whole, for that matter, but something about those lines just resonated with me, especially when I read Callie's thoughts. What a difference it would have made, I think, if she had been given the ability to see herself as others saw her.

I think that's one of the toughest things we have to go through when we're growing up. Accepting ourselves. I could never say I was perfect. I'd had my share of troubles when I was in high school.

Callie and I were both enrolled in Napier Girls' High School. I was never really the academic type and I hated school, for the most part. I enjoyed my science classes and later realised I had an aptitude for it, but the rest was just torture. My grades in all my other classes were fair, but I was never what anyone could consider a genius.

Callie had always hated it when I talked that way.

"Let's face it," I sighed to Callie one afternoon, after I'd had an argument with my mother about my poor grades. I was passing my classes, but just barely scraping through. Science was another matter. "I'm just not smart enough."

"Don't say that!" Callie told me, frowning. "You are smart. Look at your grades in science."

"According to my mother, I will never achieve anything in life with high grades in science."

"Well, your mum is wrong. Look at all the scientists out there. I mean, you could be anything you want to be," she insisted. "Not like me. I mean, what use are good grades in English and maths?" she added, tossing her report on the bed. "They're just normal subjects. What kind of job can I get with that?"

I shook my head at her. "You're the one who can be anything you want to be. I bet ... I bet if they did an I.Q test, like they do in America, you'd be like a genius."

"Nah, I'd be Forrest, Forrest Gump," she joked, quoting the line from one of our favourite movies, putting on the same slow intonation the actor had used in the movie.

I shoved her. "You're a jerk," I told her.

She poked her tongue out at me. "Takes one to know one, funny face."

I shoved her again and she shoved back until we were pretending to wrestle on the bed, trying to tickle each other. We were giggling hysterically, getting out of breath. We lay on the bed, trying to get out breath back. Finally, she sat up, her expression turning serious as she picked up the now creased paper showing my grades.

"I don't know why you think you're not smart, just because you're barely passing English. I mean, I don't get why people think that grades are like a way of showing how smart you are. Some people show they're smart in other ways."

I used to wonder what she meant by that, but I think I understand now. Intelligence shouldn't be something measured by a letter or a percentage. Some people tested well, while others just seemed to flake when it came to their tests. That didn't mean they weren't smart.

Callie always had a different way of looking at things, like a perspective on the world that was truly unique. It was one of the things that made her special.

I was reading another journal, from our second year of high school. We'd both sort of drifted apart a little, not that we could ever really get so far apart that we could give up our friendship, but by then we'd formed new friendships and were in different classes so we didn't spend as much time together as we liked. I was fourteen, almost fifteen and, according to my mother, able to be trusted in the house on my own. I think there was an unwritten rule somewhere that you had to be at least fourteen before you could be allowed at home alone.

There was one passage in the journal which disturbed me.

I was hanging out with Linda today. She's nice, although nothing like Janet. She doesn't make me laugh like Janet does. I miss Janet, but I know she's busy with her classes and her new friends.

I sometimes wonder why people are friends with me. I mean, do they really like me or is it just that they're tolerating me. I mean, Janet and I have been friends since we were seven, but does that mean she's really my friend? I honestly don't know why she puts up with me sometimes because I must be hard work. She's always having to cheer me up.

I couldn't believe what I was reading. Callie thought I was only tolerating her? I had never thought she was hard work. Sure, she could be morose at times, but so could I. I'd had my bad days, and she'd always been there to give me a morale boost. Why couldn't she see that?

I remembered reading something about a kind of disorder — I forget the name of it — but it boiled down to the fact that certain people have a distorted view of themselves. I wondered if Callie had that same disorder, I thought, an echo of my earlier thought that she really didn't see herself the way others saw her.

I carried on reading. My clock was showing almost midnight but I just had to keep going.

Anyway, Linda and I have been having problems with these girls. They're bullies, plain and simple. I really, really hate them. The other day I was in class and one of them stole the key tag off my pencil case. When I asked them to give it back they tried to tell me it was theirs. It's like years ago when there was this girl I hung out with. I had brought a game to school but it wasn't in my bag when I got home. I knew she'd stolen it, as she went in my bag for some reason, and I confronted her about it. She got all defensive and reckoned I was accusing her of stealing. She gave it back, but I was so mad I never talked to her again.

Well, so Linda and I were just sitting around talking at lunchtime and these girls started taunting us, throwing food at us, and then I heard them say something about Janet. How she was a dirty Maori and a dirty black bitch and I was so, so angry that I stalked up to them and shouted at them: how dare they say something so horrible about my best friend?

I don't care what Janet looks like. I love her like she's my sister. Who cares what the colour of her skin is?

I was horrified as I read the passage. Callie had not only confronted them about what they'd said but threatened them. I had never heard of her being so angry before. From what I'd already read, she could take a lot of things. She could take the bullying on herself, but when it came to her friends she clearly wasn't going to tolerate anything bad said about them.

Back when we were about twelve, our class had been doing a project on prejudice. They showed a movie about a school that started a sort of cult. Anyone who didn't follow the same philosophies of that cult was considered an outcast. It started to become kind of militant, with some students threatening physical violence on anyone who spoke out against it. Two students became so horrified over it that they chose to leave, even knowing that their own lives would be in danger. Toward the end of the movie, the teacher who had orchestrated the whole thing told the followers they would hear from their 'leader' at a rally, only for the leader to be revealed as Adolf Hitler. The whole thing had turned out to be an object lesson of how powerful cults could be.

Callie and I were so stunned and shocked by that

movie, we just looked at each other, our open mouths and wide eyes expressing everything we couldn't verbalise. When the teacher, toward the end of the study unit, explained about prejudice and how people who were different were treated, we just shook our heads. Maybe we were naïve to think that no one could ever treat us differently, even though we looked so different ourselves, because we cared about each other so much.

There had been another girl in the class who was kind of shy and quiet, but there were a couple of bullies in the class who treated her like a loser. At the end of the unit, the teacher asked us to write feedback, but to make it anonymous. She read some of them out in class and I remember the look of shock on her face as she read one particular note: *I don't need to know how to be treated like a loser because I am one.* She demanded to know who wrote the note and we all secretly thought it was this girl.

Even Callie thought so, although she had been trying to befriend the girl, who was even shyer than her, which was saying a lot.

Callie never cared about what a person looked like. It was one of the things I loved about her.

My phone rang, distracting me from my thoughts. I picked it up, answering it automatically without looking at the caller i.d. I knew who it was.

"Hi Tom," I said.

Despite my earlier thoughts that he wouldn't call again, we'd been talking infrequently over the past couple of weeks. Sometimes I would call him, but most of the time he would call me.

"Hi Janet. How are you doing?"

"I'm okay. Just sitting here reading."

"It's late to be reading."

I laughed. "It's late to be calling."

"I know. I was out with friends. We went out to the movies and I kept thinking: 'Callie would love this kind of movie'."

"What was the movie?"

"An action flick. She hated chick flicks."

"Yeah, I know. They always made her cry. She used to tell me they made her feel like such a girl."

Tom laughed. "She was a girl."

"Oh, you know what I mean."

"Yeah, I know. So what are you reading? As if I didn't know."

I'd told him about Callie's journals and how I'd been looking for answers in them. He always sounded concerned, saying that maybe I wouldn't find the answers there. That maybe Callie would never really give up all her secrets, even in a journal, but I had to see it for myself. I had to know what was going on in her head. Maybe then I could make some sense out of all of this.

"I'm up to our second year of high school. You knew she was bullied, right?"

"Yeah, I know." I'd told him that too.

"Anyway, there were these girls who were saying all this horrible stuff about me. Racist kind of stuff."

"Racist?"

"Yeah," I said. "Callie was so mad she threatened them."

He sounded shocked when he replied.

"Callie did? I mean, I knew she had a temper. She blew up at the manager once because of some idiot she had on the phone, but most of the time she was a total professional. She just didn't tolerate people like that. I never thought she would have had it in her to threaten someone though."

"That's just it, though, Tom. She could take anything but when it came to personal attacks against someone she cared about it was like she became Mr Hyde."

"I could see that," he agreed. "There was this one guy at work who treated her like crap, but she just took it, but then he started in on someone else and she told him where to get off."

That was Callie. Loyal to a fault. When she loved someone, she loved them wholeheartedly and would do anything for them.

"Um, so anyway, I ran into Miranda the other day."

I remembered the sweet girl from the funeral. She had given me an address for a gmail account and we kept in touch. She was still staying with the friend of Callie's, or so I'd heard, but I hadn't had an email from her in a week or so.

"She's still working at the local Mickey D's," he went on. "Her Mum died."

I winced. Poor Miranda. To have her mother pass away so soon after Callie must be hard for her. From the brief conversations we'd had, Miranda had relied on Callie to get her through the tough times, knowing there was no one else she could really turn to. Callie had always been a good listener. That was something else that made us so good together. I was the talker, she was the listener.

"God, that poor kid," I sighed.

Tom sighed in return. "Yeah. I took her out for dinner and we had a long talk. She's doing okay though. I think I even managed to talk her into going back to school. Well, she's thinking about it anyway. She told me Callie had always been trying to talk her into going back."

"Callie loved school," I told him. "She was the smart one of the two of us."

"I think Callie would have said otherwise," he replied. "Anyway, I don't know about you, but I think the whole grading system is a crock. I mean, some people just test well. It doesn't mean they're smarter than you."

"That's exactly what Callie used to say," I told him.

I listened as he began relating a story Callie had told him. I again had the impression that their relationship went deeper than friendship. It was hard to know what Callie thought about it, since she'd never talked about him. I remembered her saying once there had been a man she'd become friends with at work, but she'd never gone into detail.

It did make me wonder if the reason she had never said anything was because she felt more than friendship for him, but was too afraid to voice it.

CHAPTER TEN

"Janet, can you come into my office for a second?"

I frowned at Alex, but followed him out of my office and into his. He had no patients waiting and I wondered if he'd left that spot clear for this particular reason.

I'd had an inkling it was coming. Alex and my colleagues couldn't help but notice how tired I was getting, but I was still staying up late every night trying to read Callie's journals. I was still only up to the high school years, reluctant to put them down in case I missed something.

I was missing something though. My personal life was beginning to suffer because I couldn't just let it go. Callie had been gone a month and I still needed to know why it had happened.

I glanced around Alex's office. It was a cheerful room. The walls were painted cream but posters were scattered all around. Most doctors' offices had information posters and pamphlets but Alex thought since a lot of his patients were young children, he should make his office more about them.

Some of his patients had given him drawings the children had done. Not all of them were brilliant, but Alex treated them all like they were works of art. His patients loved him for it.

Alex was a sweet man. He had been a doctor for at least thirty years. I'd asked him once why he hadn't taken a job in a hospital but he told me he liked the personal touch. He liked being a part of his patients' lives, seeing them grow from tiny infants to adults. He had a few patients like that, most of whom now had families of their own.

His wife was just the nicest kind of woman you could ever meet. She and Alex had met in high school and the couple had been together ever since. Betty was petite and pretty. Before her hair had started to go grey, it had been fiery red. What people said about redheads was true in her case. She had a temper, but I'd only ever seen her lose her temper a couple of times, and both times it was completely justified.

I'd seen her face down a man who was at least a foot taller than her, and then some, only for him to cower before her, suitably chastened. He'd been berating the clinic receptionist about something which had not been her fault at all, and Betty had given it right back to him telling him he had no business talking to anyone that way. The sight of this diminutive redhead talking to a man who towered over her like he was a five-year-old was hilarious. He slunk away, looking completely mortified that not only had she cut him down to size, but that people were there to witness his shame.

Betty had invited me to a barbecue at their place the first year I started working at the clinic. She'd also invited a friend of hers who was single and we'd ended up going out for a few months. The relationship didn't work out but Betty kept on trying to matchmake. Not because she thought I needed a man, since I'm fairly independent, but because she thought people shouldn't be alone.

I wasn't surprised to find Betty in Alex's office. She got up from the couch where she'd been sitting and wrapped her arms around me in a motherly hug.

"You poor thing," she said.

Alex looked kindly at me.

"Janet, I know you've been having a tough time lately. We're not here to lecture you or tell you off. The truth is, we're worried about you. You're exhausted and I know you're not sleeping."

"I know," I said softly, nodding.

"Sweetheart, we just want to know you're okay," Betty said.

"I'm okay. I just ... it's been hard."

"She was your best friend and I know you feel the loss deeply," Alex said. He spoke in a gentle tone, full of sympathy. Maybe he didn't understand what I was going through, but it didn't matter. He was coming from the perspective of a doctor concerned at what it was doing to my health.

"There is nothing wrong with feeling that way, but pretending that you don't isn't helping the situation either."

I gazed at the two of them. It seemed like they were telling me to do something about it but it was like I was suddenly disconnected from my body. I knew it was the stress I was feeling. I had no idea what I was supposed to do. I loved my job, but the last thing I wanted to do was let them down.

I finally managed to gather my wits about me.

"What do you want me to do?" I asked slowly.

"We think you need to take some time off. Just for a month or so," Betty replied, her voice soft and full of motherly concern.

"A month?" I asked, hearing my voice squeak a little. "I can't take a month off! What about the clients?"

"We can get someone in to do your work, Janet," Alex said gently. "You need to look after yourself right now."

"You could go spend some time with your dad," Betty suggested. "Get some fresh air on the farm."

That was a good idea. I was certainly tempted. I still felt I owed it to the clients to stay.

"Janet," Betty said, putting her arm around my shoulder. "We really think a break would be good for you right now. You're tired and emotional and we think you need time to process it all."

I hadn't cried at work at all, but that was only because I had gotten used to hiding my emotions. She had made a good point though. I was spending all my time trying to make sense of it all and I was neglecting myself. I might not have looked it from the outside, but inside I was a mess, struggling to even get out of bed in the mornings.

I had been so one-track minded on the journals I was in denial about what it was doing to me personally.

"You're right," I admitted. "I think maybe I do

need the break."

Alex smiled. "Good girl. We've cleared your calendar for the rest of the day and we'll get someone in next week. Just promise us you will get some rest."

"I will," I said, feeling a little guilty.

Betty must have seen the emotion in my expression as she hugged me again.

"Don't you ever feel guilty for feeling like this. You're a strong person, Janet, but sometimes things can just get a little overwhelming. And you know you can come and talk to us if you're ever feeling that way."

I nodded, hugging her back before getting up and going to the door. I turned and looked back at them, offering a small smile. It was nice to know that I had a boss who genuinely did care about his staff. Unlike poor Callie, I thought.

I gathered my things and left the clinic, knowing Alex would tell the rest of the staff in the meeting on Monday. He always held the staff meeting at the beginning of the week so anyone with any concerns from the week before could discuss them and maybe get opinions from the rest of the team.

The clinic had six GPs, other than Alex, and as many nurses. Aside from myself taking care of physiotherapy, there was also a small lab, an optometrist, a podiatrist and a massage therapist who was only open three days a week. Betty was the clinic's administrator and took care of the accounts.

It was a small team of about twenty-five and we were all very close. Every one of them were consummate professionals who worked hard and loved their jobs. I had no doubt when Alex told them why I was taking a short leave of absence they would be very concerned. Unlike Callie's office, I thought again.

Tom had told me that he'd noticed Callie had been very down about a month before her death. The company where she worked was part of a larger company. Her division was fairly small, although it still had about twice as many staff as the clinic, and from what Tom had said, the staff didn't really care that much about each other. They worked in teams but only because they were forced to.

The only person who did seem to care was the division manager, Kim, Tom had told me.

Callie had been left on her own to do her job, with no help when things got overwhelming. Tom had been furious on her behalf when she'd broken down crying and her team leader hadn't even bothered to find out what was wrong. She'd basically been told to just deal with whatever it was and stop acting like a child.

The morning Callie died, Tom had immediately noticed her absence. No matter how much Callie hated her job, she had always been so conscientious and had made sure she was at work early. When she wasn't at her desk that morning, he'd been worried.

I'd spent some time that horrible morning searching through Callie's contacts list on her cellphone, trying to identify her boss, figuring she'd at least have that stored so if anything happened to her anyone would know who to contact. The list wasn't huge, but I still hadn't relished the thought of going through it to find out who needed to know urgently.

It was a difficult task, but Susan had still been too

emotional. I'd always been more pragmatic, able to focus on doing what had to be done even when it felt like everything was falling apart. There was no getting out of it, I'd told myself. They had to know.

I'd called the first two on the list. They were understandably shocked at the news, but couldn't help with any information about her job. I was just about to dial the third number when the phone rang. It had been switched off as it had run out of battery power but I'd charged it so I could go through the contacts.

"Hello, this is Janet."

The voice that answered me was abrupt and almost aggressive. I instantly didn't like the man.

"I'm looking for Callie. This is Callie's phone, isn't it?"

"Um, yes, it is."

"Is she sick? Is that why she's not at work?" The man sounded extremely annoyed, although that was putting it mildly. He had an accent which I couldn't quite place.

"I'm sorry, who is this?"

"This is Phillip. Her team leader. Who are you?" he asked abruptly.

"Uh, Phillip, my name is Janet. I'm, uh, a close friend of Callie's."

"Well, put her on."

"I can't."

"Why not?" he barked.

I bit my lip. It was late morning and it had already been a long day. I'd been up almost nine hours after only about four hours' sleep and I was so tired it hurt to even think.

"I'm very sorry to have to tell you this, Phillip, but Callie died this morning."

"Is this some kind of a joke?" he asked rudely.

I swallowed a lump in my throat. Part of me wanted to tell him off for speaking so rudely to me, but another part of me could understand why he would think that.

"No, sir, it's no joke. Callie died early this morning."

The phone conversation was rather short after that. He didn't even thank me for the information and hung up once I'd told him I would let him know when all the details had been finalised.

Once I'd got off the phone I understood why Callie hadn't liked him. He had what Alex would call a lousy bedside manner.

Tom and I had talked about that phone call. He told me that Phillip had got up from his desk, strode angrily down toward the manager's office and walked in without knocking. The team leader's annoyance had been clear to everyone in the office and they knew something was up.

Callie might have been quiet in the office, but while no one could say they were close friends with her, apart from Tom, they all knew her well enough to know she wouldn't just abandon her job. The fact that she wasn't in the office and hadn't called to say she was sick didn't bode well.

Tom had observed the team leader getting more and more agitated when he'd tried to get through to Callie's phone, with no luck. More than once the man had growled that Callie 'better have a good excuse for not being at work or else there would be hell to pay'. There was not even a hint of concern that something might have happened to her.

As far as Tom was concerned, Phillip was nothing short of a bully. In his personal opinion, the man was threatened by Callie, who was clearly much smarter than he was. Then again, he thought everyone was smarter than Phillip. God only knew why the man was a team leader, he told me. He'd often watched the way Phillip would talk to Callie, doing his best to put her down. Tom had tried talking to her about confronting her team leader, but she'd always been too afraid.

Phillip had only been in the job a few months, whereas Callie had been there for five years, still in the same position she had been hired for. It wasn't fair, I thought. Callie worked harder than anyone I knew, even if she wasn't happy doing what she did, yet she always seemed to miss out on promotions.

Tom had watched Phillip walk out of the office and go back to his desk, still looking extremely annoyed and agitated. Five minutes later, Kim, the manager, sent an email around calling everyone in to an urgent meeting.

They'd assembled in the board room, wondering what was going on. Kim, a woman in her forties, looked pale and shaken as she faced them.

She took a deep breath and let it out slowly.

"I have some sad news to share with you. Callie passed away this morning."

There were some shocked gasps and Tom had looked around at everyone. Some of them seemed to be completely devastated, while a couple of them just seemed to have smug expressions on their faces. Tom glared at the two culprits.

"What happened?" Tom asked, his voice shaky with emotion.

"I don't know all the details," Kim said, still looking very upset. Tom knew Kim had liked Callie. "All I know is that it was very sudden. They're still finalising the details for the funeral so I don't have any information on that yet." She sighed. "In the meantime, if you could please just respect the family's wishes for privacy."

Rumours had begun flying around the office and a couple of people had made some snide comments about Callie, which had made Tom so angry he had wanted to punch someone. He'd been so devastated when he'd learned that Callie had killed herself. He'd quietly confessed to me that he'd wanted to have it out with Callie's team leader, even though he knew it wouldn't change anything.

It wasn't fair. Callie hadn't deserved that sort of treatment and even in death it seemed she couldn't escape it. But that was the difference between my work and hers. I had a job I loved and colleagues I got along well with and could count on. It just wasn't fair.

CHAPTER ELEVEN

I stopped in at my mother's place before I went home. Mum had only just got home from work herself, but my stepfather was still working. Mum was forever telling him he needed to cut down his hours, but I think he liked keeping busy.

Mum and my stepfather, Bill, have been together since I was a teenager. He's a very sweet man who puts her first, no matter what. In many ways, her second marriage was better than her first because I noticed an intimacy between them that I never really saw with my parents. It was in the non-verbals, I thought, where they could look at each other and not have to say a word to know what the other is thinking.

"Hi honey," Mum called out.

"Hi Mum," I said, putting my bag down on the couch and going to find her in the study. She was sitting at the computer typing an email to a friend. She stopped typing and turned in her chair to look at me.

Mum didn't look like a woman in her late fifties. I've seen some women who looked old before their time but not my mother. Her blonde hair had turned kind of ash-blonde with age, but her skin still looked youthful. I always hoped when I got to her age I would be just as youthful-looking.

She was not the type of person who went to the gym, but she still kept herself in shape by going out for long walks every night with Bill. When they went shopping at the local shopping mall, he was always holding her hand. I used to be a little embarrassed by how 'mushy' they could be, when I was a teenager at least, but now I don't mind the affectionate gestures. It made her happy and that was all that mattered.

In many ways, Bill was a better husband to my mum than my dad was. I was too young to ever really analyse my parents relationship in detail before the divorce, but I did get the sense that they were much happier apart and better being friends than husband and wife.

Her blue eyed gaze was a little disconcerting as she studied me, a frown furrowing her brow.

"You look tired, sweetie," she said, with obvious concern.

"I'm fine Mum."

She shook her head, her shoulder-length hair catching the late afternoon sun shining through the windows of the study.

"No, you're not. I know when something's upset you."

"I'm not upset," I replied. "I just ... Alex and Betty told me to take some time off work."

Her frown deepened.

"Why would they do that? Are they unhappy with your work?"

"No, Mum. They're just concerned, I guess."

Mum rose from her chair and went out to the kitchen. I followed her, watching as she put the kettle on. It had clearly not long boiled as it didn't take long to boil more water and she grabbed two sachets of flavoured coffee, giving me the Caramel Latte one.

We sat at the kitchen table, pretty ceramic mugs set on coasters in front of us. Mum had bought a set of the floral decorated cups on sale. She always seemed to have an uncanny ability to find anything on sale and pick it up for a bargain.

"So, why are they concerned?" she asked. "Is it because of Callie?"

I nodded. "I've been reading her journals every night, trying to figure out why she did it."

"Oh honey, you shouldn't …"

"I have to know Mum. You know how Callie and I felt about each other. She was my best friend and now she's gone and I don't understand why."

My voice broke and I swallowed hard, trying to get rid of the lump in my throat. Mum put a hand on top of mine.

"Honey, you need to let this go. Callie wouldn't want you to suffer like this."

"I can't help it. I need to know. I need to know if there's something I did, or something I could have done to prevent it."

She stared at me for a long moment, her brow furrowed in worry and sympathy.

"Janet, what do you think you could have done?" she asked quietly. "Why are you blaming yourself for this?"

"I just think maybe if I'd talked to her, been there for her ..."

"You were there for her. This is not your fault."

I stood up, feeling anger boiling over.

"So what? Do I blame her instead? Cry and scream about how selfish she was to leave? Do you think I haven't?"

Mum had tears in her eyes.

"Oh sweetie, no!"

"But she is selfish. She didn't think about how hard it would be for those left behind. Me and ... and Tom."

"Baby, you need to let this go," she repeated. "This is hurting you."

Mum didn't understand, but then, how could she possibly understand the pain I was feeling. I was angry at Callie. Part of me wanted to hate her for what she did, for leaving me this way. A big part of me knew it was wrong to feel that way, but another part understood that it was just part of the grieving process. But how could I hate my best friend?

I left Mum's shortly after dinner, although I had little appetite and just pushed the food around on my plate. Mum and Bill tried to coax me to eat but I could barely stomach it. I guessed this was one of the things Alex was worried about. I'd lost a little weight over the past month.

That night I called Tom. He seemed to be the only person who understood what I was feeling.

"A whole month?" he asked, sounding surprised when I told him about the meeting with my boss.

"Yeah, I guess they were worried about me."

"Well, I can't say I'm surprised," he said. "You

have been a little obsessed with Callie's diaries lately."

"Tom, you know why I'm doing this."

"I know," he sighed, "but I worry. I worry that you're spending too much time trying to figure this out and not giving yourself time to grieve."

"I just … I need to know. It hurts, Tom. It hurts that she was so selfish. I mean, I know it's wrong to feel this way."

"What? To be angry at her for doing it? Janet, it's normal. Please, trust me on this."

"How do you know?" I asked.

"I had this friend. He was a lot like Callie. He tended to brood a lot and spend an awful lot of time by himself and I never knew why. One day I confronted him. Asked him what his problem was. Totally the wrong thing to say. He got so angry at me he hit me. A week later he was dead. He'd hung himself off a bridge. Not long after he died, I was talking to another friend of his and he told me that my friend had been sexually abused when he was a kid. By his uncle. Well, he wasn't really his uncle. He was a friend of the family. I never knew, because he never told me what he went through." He paused.

"I'm not saying this is what Callie went through, but … look, all I'm saying is, you can be close to someone but never really know what's going through their head. As much as it hurts to say, maybe this was just something Callie felt she couldn't talk to you about."

"But we were close, Tom. She was as close to me as if she was my sister. I think I would know …"

"I have a sister, and I don't tell her everything. I

was there the other day and she was asking me what was going on in my life. I never told her about Callie."

Surely it was different for brothers and sisters, I thought.

"I don't know Tom," I said.

"Janet, don't do this to yourself. You have to let her go. She wouldn't want this."

I felt an irrational anger bubble up from inside and the need to lash out. Even though a big part of me knew he was right. It was the same thing my mother had told me a few hours earlier, but I didn't like hearing it.

"How do you know what she would have wanted? You barely knew her! Her own flatmate ..."

Tom was quiet for a moment and I guessed he was letting me get my anger out.

"I don't want to sound like I'm blaming her for it, but the truth is, Callie never shared herself with anyone. I would have helped her in a heartbeat if she'd just come to me, but she was too proud."

It did sound like he was blaming her, but it was no more than what I had done myself. I was just so ... angry! If she'd just talked to me, I would have understood. I never judged her. I never thought she was a loser.

God, Callie, why didn't you talk to me? Why did you have to leave me in such pain?

Tom continued talking. He spoke kindly and I could hear the concern in his voice.

"Callie's been gone a month and it feels like ever since you've just become ... I don't know. I mean, when I met you, you were like ... you were different. I feel like you're slipping away and I'm worried."

"I wish you wouldn't."

"Not worry about you? I like worrying about you."

I wrinkled my nose, then laughed. "That is such a weird thing to say."

"Got you laughing though," he said and I laughed again. There was something about him that always made me feel better.

For a few moments we didn't speak. It wasn't an uncomfortable silence. I wasn't sure what it was, but Tom was the first man I knew where I could just sit and not have to say anything.

"You know," he said, after a few minutes, "if you're at a loose end, I mean, since you have the next month off work, why don't you come up here? You could stay at my place. I have a spare room."

I bit my lip. Tom sounded like a nice guy and we'd had some good chats over the phone, but that was over the phone, not in person.

Still, it probably would do me some good to have a change of scenery. Get out of my own head, so to speak.

"I promise I'm not an axe murderer," Tom cajoled and I couldn't help laughing again at his tone. I could see why he and Callie had got along so well. They seemed to have the same sense of humour.

"Look, if it's the city you're worried about, don't. I promise, it really isn't that bad once you get to know the place. And there are some nice sights around here. At least come and stay for a week. I can take a week off work and just show you around."

"All right," I agreed. "I'm gonna go see my dad for a

couple of days but I can come up after that."

"How about next Wednesday?" he said. "There's a basketball game on Wednesday night and I know you love basketball." I'd told him that in one of our conversations. "It's not much fun going on your own."

"Okay," I replied, pretending to sigh heavily. "You twisted my arm."

After I hung up from Tom, I took the latest journal to bed and sat up reading. It was just after Callie had left high school. She had been having arguments with her parents over getting a job, but without qualifications there wasn't much she could really go for and she didn't want a minimum wage job. She really wanted to go to university, but there was just not the money.
Getting a student loan was apparently out of the question.

Mum wants me to go but she doesn't want me to get a loan. Dad doesn't think I'll be able to finish. I even suggested maybe even going for an apprenticeship in cabinet making but he said that wasn't a career for a girl. He's so backward sometimes. Like girls can't build things. What does he know? I loved woodworking at school, but I had to take subjects like typing and economic studies.

Janet told me she's going to do a one-year diploma at uni and then think about where she goes from there. She's thinking something along the lines of being a nurse or something. I'm so jealous. Her parents support her but mine ... it's like they don't trust me or something. I'm tired of it.

I found out something. My parents got married because they had to. Mum was pregnant with me and her parents told her there was no way they were going to let her bring me up alone. I haven't told them I know. I only found out because I looked up when my parents got married and compared it with my birthday. They lied about their real wedding date, but it was all there in the records. I was born six months later. There was no way I could have been that premature, so why did they lie?

Did my parents even want me? I don't know. I get the feeling sometimes they wish I was never born. God knows, they probably would have been happier without me around.

Sometimes I wonder if my parents ever really loved each other. They're always fighting over something and I can't stand it. I know Dad hates it that Mum can earn more than he ever could in his job. I heard them once, fighting about money. He basically accused my grandparents of looking down on him because he wasn't as smart or didn't come from the right background.

I couldn't read any more. It hurt too much to think that Callie was going through this for so many years and she'd never said a word.

CHAPTER TWELVE

Before I left for my dad's place, there was one thing I wanted to clear up. At least in my own mind.

Marion and Richard James lived in a fairly modest two-bedroom weatherboard house on the west side of town. Richard spent much of his time keeping the property clean and tidy, but was forever complaining, especially in autumn, about the leaves that kept falling off the trees. He claimed it was a hassle cleaning them up all the time and wished the council would just get rid of the trees.

I recalled an incident when Callie and I had been teenagers. She had been learning about the environment. It had become one of her passions, or rather, one of her obsessions. Callie had had the kind of personality in which she would find something that piqued her interest, but it would burn out quickly. She always seemed to have half a dozen projects that had sat unfinished.

Not this, though. The environment was one of those few subjects which seemed to ignite her passion and keep it. She had wanted to join an organisation like

Greenpeace years ago, but her parents had talked her out of it.

I used to get the impression that her parents didn't trust her. I suppose in many ways they were just waiting for her to drop the interest as she did so many other things.

She had told me once she had an argument with her father over his complaints about the trees. While she had never shown an aptitude for science, somehow this was the one thing that had always stuck with her, explaining to her father that trees not only beautified the landscape but they had their environmental uses, launching into a long-winded explanation about the roots and photosynthesis.

What had upset her the most was the way her father had laughed at her, as if he hadn't taken her seriously.

"It's just the same as when I said I wanted to take woodwork at school. He thought that was all a huge joke."

Richard seemed to be an old-fashioned man. I wouldn't have gone so far as to call him sexist, although in many ways that was what he was. Women had their jobs and men had theirs and never the twain shall meet, was pretty much his philosophy.

He was out in the front yard as I pulled up and parked on the road, weeding the flower garden. Marion was rather proud of her garden. It had taken a few years and a lot of money for it to look as good as it was. It had once featured in a newspaper article when garden shows were all the rage. Marion kept the article in a scrapbook and liked to bring it out to show visitors once in a while.

She often despaired of Callie ever developing a green thumb. It wasn't that Callie wasn't a gardener; it was just that Callie had never had a place of her own and the time to dedicate to gardening. I'd noticed that about a lot of people these days. They often talked about a work-life balance but most people were too busy trying to keep their heads above water, working long hours just to make ends meet, to worry about having a life afterward.

Richard stopped working and straightened up as I walked up the driveway.

"Hello Janet," he said quietly.

He seemed somehow smaller, greyer, as if Callie's death had taken a toll on him. I was a few metres away but I could see there was no life in his eyes.

It struck me that this was a man who was not only grieving for his only child, but also that his heart was heavy. Did he blame himself for what Callie had done?

I remembered his words in the funeral home when we'd been viewing Callie's body. 'I'm sorry'. What was he sorry for?

"Mr James," I said, not knowing whether to reach out and hug him.

Ever since I'd known Callie's family, they had never been an affectionate family. There were few hugs, if any. It was one thing that differed vastly from my own family. My father was big on hugging. Often embarrassingly so; at least when I was a teenager. My mother was not quite so demonstrative when she was younger, but even now when she and my dad see each other, they hug and kiss like friends.

Richard held out his hand and I took it. The

handshake was weak and almost lifeless. It was a gesture of courtesy, nothing more. It was as if I was a stranger, rather than someone he'd known for over twenty years.

He gestured toward the house and I followed him inside. Marion was sitting at the table, working on some project. She always had various art projects she was working on. I gathered that was where Callie had got that from. My friend had always told me it irritated her father when he saw Marion's projects spread all over the table. She always wondered why, if it bothered him so much, he didn't work on something for himself. He never really seemed to have any interest outside of working on the property.

Marion looked up at me and smiled. She seemed to be taking things better than Richard. I'd always had the impression that she was stronger than her husband.

"Hello Janet. How are you doing?"

"I'm okay. I'm sorry I haven't been by in a while."

"No, it's okay," Marion assured me, shaking her head. "I'm sure you've been busy with work. Would you like a coffee?"

"Thanks," I said, fighting the urge to shove my hands in my pockets.

Marion looked at Richard and he nodded.

"I'll just go and put the kettle on," he said, sighing.

I could feel the tension in the room, as if suddenly all the warm air had been sucked out. It wasn't frigid, but it was getting there. I realised there was some sort of undercurrent in this house. Whether it had been there before Callie died was hard to say. All I knew was that this marriage was in deep trouble.

Marion invited me to sit down at the table and cleared some of her papers so there was a space for me to put a cup down. We talked for a little while about work and whether or not I had anyone special in my life. We kept to trivial subjects, neither one of us really wanting to discuss the huge elephant in the room.

It was inevitable anyway.

Richard returned with three mugs of coffee, the aroma reminding me a little of the cafes I had visited as a child when I'd gone shopping with my mother. We used to have a little ritual where we would go to the local mall, get our shopping done, then sit down at the mall café for a bite to eat and a coffee. Well, Mum would have the coffee and I would have a milkshake.

Richard had barely said a word since he'd come in the house with me. As he sat down at the table, I saw the older couple exchange glances, then both sighed deeply.

I touched the mug, running my finger up and down the china, careful of the hot contents.

"Uh, there's something I … I wanted to talk to you. About Callie."

"What is it?" Marion asked.

"I've been reading her … her journals. Something came up in one of the entries. I wanted to ask you about it."

I hesitantly told them about the entry where Callie had described going to the library and looking through the microfiche; her discovery of her parents' real marriage date. Richard did not look happy as I related all this and glanced at his wife.

Marion also looked unhappy, but resigned.

"Yes, it's true. We lied about the date we got married. We didn't want Callie to think that the only reason we got married was because I was pregnant."

I nodded. It was fairly clear there had already been issues because of it.

"Callie came to us a few years ago and told us she knew, just knew, that we only got married because of her," Richard told me. "She kept blaming herself for the way things were, saying if we'd never had her then things would have been easier."

"Was she right?"

Marion looked at me, her eyebrows shooting up in surprise.

"Goodness no. No matter what she thought, we would never ever think that about her. We loved her. Janet, we were engaged long before Callie was even a twinkle in her father's eye, and that's the truth. We just realised we had to move up the wedding date, that's all."

Richard glanced at his wife again and there seemed to be something unspoken between them.

"I really wish there was a simple explanation for what happened to Callie," he said. "The truth is I blame myself for it."

"Why?" I asked.

"Because a week before she ... we had a fight. You know Callie and I were always close ..." He broke off.

Marion touched my hand. "Callie and her father were very much alike in temperament. They clashed a lot of the time."

"What was the fight about?"

"It doesn't matter," Richard said, shaking his head.

"I just know I upset her."

"No," Marion said softly. "You can't keep blaming yourself for this. Remember what the counsellor said."

"Counsellor?" I asked.

"We've been seeing a counsellor once a week," Richard explained. "To try and make sense of all of this. To save ..." He looked at Marion once again. "... our marriage."

I understood. My earlier feelings about them were right. Their marriage was in trouble, but at least they were doing something about it. They were both still in so much pain, although Marion was clearly better at hiding it than her husband.

I realised I was right about Richard. It wasn't just the fight they'd had before Callie died. I had the feeling that he kept beating himself up over little things, like never encouraging Callie to do what she wanted to do, making her feel like he wouldn't love her if she chose something he didn't think she was capable of doing.

I left them an hour or so later, feeling happier at least that I had managed to clear up some of the things I had been thinking.

They'd lied to protect their daughter from the stigma of being conceived out of wedlock. That was a bad decision on their part, and clearly Callie had taken it the wrong way.

It still bothered me a little that Callie could think so badly of herself. That she would blame herself for the problems her parents had, when they were really nothing to do with her.

Marion and Richard blamed themselves for that too, which was sad. There was too much blaming going

around. God knew I was guilty of that as well

CHAPTER THIRTEEN

I left for Te Kuiti early the next morning, wanting to avoid as much of the highway traffic as possible. My hometown was quite small in comparison to other towns, but then again it was mostly a farming town. There was a reason it's called the 'shearing capital' of the world.

Callie, being the city kid she was, was funny whenever she visited the farm. I could still recall the first time she came and my father was teasing her about the fact she had never milked a cow before, and never knew what went on at a sheep farm, which was the next farm over. We were primarily dairy.

Her face was a picture when he told her what they did to the lambs when they were still young.

"Why?" she said, her eyes huge. "Isn't it cruel?"

"No crueller than letting flies lay their eggs in the lamb's tail," Dad pointed out.

"They do that?" she asked. "Ewww!"

That was her introduction to the world of farming. Dad went to help a neighbour when they had to do the docking and came back with a tail, teasing her with it.

I knew it was kind of silly, but she really didn't know much about farming at all. She once said to me she didn't really want to know where her meat came from.

I supposed some people would have hated farmers like my dad because it did seem like a pretty cruel practice, but it was the way of life. New Zealand was built on farming, at least in its first 150 years. Maybe that has changed as more people have gone to work and live in the cities.

Dad has often asked me whether I would go back to live in a farming town and I honestly couldn't say what I would do. With the amount of injuries that could occur on a farm there would always be work, but I'm comfortable where I am.

It was at least a three-and-a-half-hour drive to Te Kuiti. I decided to take my time. There was no need to rush it. Not that I wasn't looking forward to seeing my dad. The last time I had visited the farm was around Christmas, as my job kept me fairly busy and my father, unfortunately, couldn't exactly leave the farm for an extended period. Not without getting help from the neighbouring farms.

I took a break at a café just outside of Taupo. Checking my phone for the time, I saw that Tom had sent me a text.

Hi, just wanted to see how you were doing. Guess you're on your way to your dad's. Having a quiet weekend. You're still coming up on Wednesday, right?

He'd attached a silly smilie which made me laugh. I didn't know what it was, but each time I talked to him I got a nice, tingly sort of feeling. He was kind and funny and h really seemed to care how I was doing.

The last guy I felt that way about had turned out to be a not so nice guy after all. Stephen had been my age. We'd met when I'd gone to the movies one night. He had been sitting in the row behind me. The theatre hadn't been full, but then the movie had been one of those film festival types which weren't popular with the younger crowd.

I'd become bored halfway through the film but since I had shelled out for the ticket, I figured I would give it a chance. It seemed Stephen had been just as bored as he jumped over the seat and sat next to me.

"Is it me or is this film mind-numbingly dull?" he asked.

"Yeah, it's boring," I said.

We talked back and forth for a while, making fun of various incidents in the movie, laughing at the inanity of it. We talked so much we hardly noticed when the film ended.

He asked me out to dinner next week, suggesting another film we could see which we could also make fun of.

We dated for about six months and things seemed to be going nicely, until I was out to dinner with friends one night at the local bar and grill. I saw him with a pretty blonde girl looking fairly intimate. It was fairly clear they were more than just friends.

When I confronted him about it, he tried to justify it by saying we'd never been exclusive, but I'd never been so angry in my life. I told him I never wanted to see him again.

So maybe I did have those initial feelings of attraction for Tom. I didn't know how he felt and even if I did, I would rather take things slowly.

I sent him a text back, telling him I was fine, and I was still coming. I was looking forward to it. As much as I disliked Auckland, I did want to get out of my place for a while. I thought a change of scenery might actually help, especially when I was still trying to work out some of the issues that had cropped up in my reading of Callie's journals.

It was early afternoon by the time I neared the outskirts of town. Te Kuiti was surrounded by steep hills which, at this time of year, were more muddy than green. It rained a lot in winter.

As I drove along the highway, I could see the gorse on one side of the road, and rolling pastures on the other. Gorse was pretty much considered a pest of a plant. It was introduced by settlers in the very early days of European settlement and was one of those noxious weeds that just seemed to spread, no matter what they tried. Even my father despaired of ever getting rid of all the gorse on the land.

Still, even that reminded me a little of 'home'. What is that saying? You can take the kid off the farm, but you can never take the farm out of the kid? Or something like that. That was the way I felt about it, in many ways. Not that I could ever see myself being a farmer. Dad would never push that on me either, even though I was an only child. He was a big believer in letting people choose their own path in life.

His family weren't exactly farmers either. At least, not on my grandmother's side; not in recent family history anyway. I didn't know if I could say the Maori side of the family were farmers either, but they did have a long tradition of working the land. Just not, I suppose, what the European side would call farming.

As I passed the sign for the scenic reserve, the feeling of being home intensified. There was a peace about being in the country that I could never seem to find in the city.

When I was a kid, not long after Mum moved to Napier, I would spend summer holidays with my dad on the farm. Callie used to ask me what I did and I always told her I would help feed the cows or clean out the stalls. Maybe I didn't do a great job, since at age seven and eight I wasn't that tall, or strong, but I still enjoyed it. My father and I would take a rake each and work side by side and he'd talk to me about my life in the city and then tell me all the gossip around town. It was nice.

I often recall with amusement the tall tales my father used to tell Callie when she visited. We'd once had a neighbour, Artie Johnson, who was about two metres tall. Callie had been amazed. She wasn't used to seeing men that tall, even though her parents were slightly above average height themselves.

Artie had come over one afternoon for something or other, and Dad had invited him to have a beer. There was nothing my father liked more than a bottle of ice cold beer on a hot day.

The two of them sat out on the porch, basically shooting the breeze, while Callie and I sat on the porch swing, drinking Cokes, and just listening to the conversation. I noticed her looking at Artie curiously.

"How did you get so tall?" she asked.

Before Artie could say anything, my father winked

at him and replied:

"Artie fell into a cow pat when he was a young'un. Face first." He clapped one hand against the other. "Splat!"

Callie's widened. "He didn't!" she said.

Artie grinned. "Yup. Came home with a face full of muck. Used to go out on cold mornings and stand barefoot in the cow pat. Best way to warm your feet up."

Callie made a face. Dad and I hid our laughter.

One Saturday, Dad made a boil-up. It's kind of a tradition among some Maori families, although most preferred a hangi, which is a method of cooking which dates back centuries. They dig a pit and heat stones before putting them in the pit and then putting the food in the pit with the hot stones and burying it for several hours.

A boil-up was different and it sort of depended on what people put in it. My dad liked to put in bacon bones, with kumara and pumpkin, along with these sort of dumplings. Some people called them doughboys. They were like scones – which had the same ingredients – except instead of being baked they were dumped in the boiling water

I couldn't say Callie had been a fussy eater, because she usually ate everything that was put down in front of her, but she was definitely no fan of the boil-up. She screwed up her nose and refused to eat it, even when I told her, not seriously of course, that she would offend my dad if she didn't eat. Dad had just shrugged philosophically.

"Not everyone's cup of tea, Chook," he had said.

I drove past the old Foster place on the right. They ran an orchard once and used to have a stall in the summer time. Callie and I had gone there once, hoping to get some good fruit, but the old man, who was probably in his eighties at the time, was a crotchety old guy and didn't take kindly to us. Even me, who he'd known since I was little. I had heard the old man had passed away about ten years ago and the family had leased the land to a neighbouring farmer, who had got rid of the orchard and decided to grow pine trees. I gathered from my dad that it wasn't too successful a venture, given there was a lot of limestone in the soil.

As I approached the bridge across the railway tracks, to drive down into the valley, a utility passed, then stopped up the road a little and began to reverse back. There were no cars behind me but I pulled off the road anyway as the driver pulled up on the other side of me and stopped.

"Well, hey Janet."

"Hey Mick," I said, smiling in greeting.

Mick was one of my dad's friends. Aged in his late forties, he reminded me a little of a man who became something of a celebrity back when I was a kid. The man did a series of tv ads for a brand of vehicle. What people liked about him wasn't just the humour in the ads, but because he was exactly the kind of man who would buy those sorts of vehicles. The man of the land type of character, who didn't care about appearance.

Mick was like that. It was hard to tell what his hair was like as it was always hidden under a bushman's type hat. He had a moustache that had turned grey, which my dad would jokingly describe as a rat's nest because it was never trimmed. His face had the ruddy look of someone who spent a lot of time in the sun.

"So, heard you were coming to spend a couple of days with the old man."

"Yeah," I said, nodding.

"You're looking good, kid. City must agree with ya."

"Sometimes, Mick," I replied. "But it's always good to come home again."

"Well don't be a stranger, eh?" he said. "Boys could do with some fresh blood round here."

I rolled my eyes and chuckled. I knew most of the 'boys' in town and they were better friends than potential dates.

"I gotta get going," I said. "Dad's expecting me."

"Might come round and have a brew one day," Mick hinted.

"I'm only here until Wednesday," I told him. "Heading up to Auckland for a few days."

Mick raised an eyebrow.

"Auckland? Whaddya wanna go to that shithole for? Ain't nothing there but city folk."

I didn't reply to that. Mick was like a lot of people who would rather stick to the country than even spend a minute more than necessary in the city. Not that his point of view was all that bad, really, but it did seem a little close-minded.

I watched him as he drove back down the road, and continued on into town. I drove past the shops along the main street — hairdresser, takeaways, cafes, real estate agency, even a supermarket, although it was not like the big city supermarkets which boasted low prices. I noticed a couple of the shops were empty —

like everywhere else, Te Kuiti had been hit by the economic problems plaguing not just the country, but everywhere else in the world.

I turned off the main street and passed the houses. There were no new buildings in town and most of the houses seemed a little sad. They clearly needed some decent maintenance.

A few minutes later I was back in the rural part of the country, off the sealed road and onto gravel. The driveway was about two hundred metres down from where the sealed road ended. I turned off and drove slowly down the winding driveway toward the farmhouse, hit by a wave of nostalgia as I saw the home of my childhood.

It was a mix of brick and weatherboard. Dad told me once his father had built an extension on the house which didn't match the rest of it, but he hadn't cared. My grandfather was always a 'do-it-yourselfer' and never took advice from anyone, no matter how well-meaning it was.

As I stopped the car on the driveway and got out to get a good look at the house, I heard a tractor rumbling behind me. I turned and smiled as Dad stopped it and turned off the engine, making sure it wasn't going anywhere before he got off and held out his arms.

"Hey Chook," he said.

I went eagerly into his arms and felt him wrap them around me. There was that familiar scent I had always loved. That outdoorsy smell, the slight muskiness of sweat from hard work, the fertiliser he used on crops and maybe just a hint of the cows.

"Welcome home, bub."

CHAPTER FOURTEEN

Dad made us both a cup of tea and we sat down at the kitchen table. He wasn't a coffee drinker. I'd asked him once and he'd said it was probably was something that harked back to his European ancestry.

My grandmother's family came from old English stock. I had never really delved into the family history that much, but I did know that my great-great something or other grandfather had been one of the first Europeans to come and settle in New Zealand around 1850 or so, a few years after the first governor had signed the treaty with the Maori.

Great Great something or other Grandfather William had been what they would have called a 'gentleman farmer' from Suffolk, or so my grandfather had once told me, but the family had fallen on hard times, which wasn't unusual in those days. He had come to New Zealand looking for a better life, leaving his wife and child behind, sending for them several months later once he had found a place to settle. He'd eventually built a place in what became our capital city – Wellington – and had started a small business.

That business eventually closed around the time of the Depression and my great grandfather, who had married a Maori girl, moved the family north, getting a job as a labourer on a small farm. My grandmother had been a teenager when she met my grandfather who had also moved north to get work as a labourer. A couple of years later he went off to join the Maori Battalion in the second World War, lying about his age to get in, since he was barely seventeen at the time.

Eventually he'd come back from the war and married my grandmother. They'd managed to scrape up enough money together to buy some land and had started a small dairy farm, which eventually became our family farm. We now had about two hundred hectares – the average size for a dairy farm.

My dad's father was in his early nineties but he still liked to work on the farm. He often said it helped keep his mind active. It was tough for a while, after my grandmother died. He still missed her even though it's been about thirty years since she passed, but he keeps busy.

"So, where's Grandad?" I asked.

"Out the back, trying to clear some of the gorse. You know your grandad. Never been afraid of hard work."

I nodded, preferring not to comment. Grandad had never let anyone else tell him what to do, or that he was too old to do something. From what I'd heard, he'd been a terror in the battalion, ending up on charges for insubordination a few times, but he'd also been known as something of a jokester.

I spooned some sugar into my tea, which was, as my

grandad, Wiremu, would often say, strong enough for the spoon to stand up in it. I never had the heart to tell my dad I didn't like my tea that strong. Most of the time I really preferred coffee. My father would probably tell me I'd become way too much of a city kid, and I supposed he had a point. Napier couldn't be called cosmopolitan, not like Auckland, but was still too 'city' for him.

"How are you doing?" he asked, watching as I stirred my tea absently.

"I'm okay."

He raised an eyebrow at me.

"Really?"

"Dad, I'm fine. Just, you know … hanging in there."

"Your mum's worried about you."

"She rang you, huh?" I asked, looking at him.

"Do you blame her? You've barely talked to anyone for weeks." He patted my arm. "Chook, I know how you felt about Callie. She was like your sister."

"I miss her. I mean, I know we didn't talk as often as we used to, but we were still close."

"I know sweetheart, but Callie wouldn't want you suffering like this."

"I just … I need to know, Dad. There had to be a reason she did what she did."

He sipped his tea, looking down at the surface of the table for a few moments. I guessed he was trying to think of something to say that wouldn't seem like a lecture.

"Janet, this isn't like you," he said seriously, finally looking at me. "You've never been one for introspection." He raised his hand before I could object. "I remember the first time I met Callie. She struck me as very shy and don't get me wrong, I could see you two really cared about each other, but I did wonder why you got along so well. You were complete opposites of each other. Not that that's a bad thing, honey. You've always been gregarious where she was shy."

I nodded. I knew he wasn't trying to be hurtful; he was just trying to understand.

"I started to realise from some of the things you used to say about Callie that she wasn't well. But I had no idea what to do or what to say to help."

"She couldn't help being sick, Dad."

"No, I know. I've been doing a bit of reading, ever since you told me she had died. I don't know everything about mental illness but I read a couple of theories that said it had something to do with a chemical imbalance in the brain."

"I know this, Dad."

He shushed me. "It's not something we've ever really talked about, you and I. Did you know your mum had post-natal depression when she had you?"

I stared at him. "What?"

He nodded. "When we first brought you home from the hospital, she didn't want to be around you. She would walk off and leave you when you started crying, saying it was getting on her nerves. Don't get me wrong, sweetheart. Your mum loves you to bits, but at the time, neither of us really understood what was happening and I have to admit I did get angry at her, thinking she was neglecting you on purpose. It never even occurred to us that she might be sick.

"Then one day, I think you were about three months old, I came home from helping Jack across the way and found her in the corner of your room, curled up in a ball. She was crying, you were crying, and she admitted to me she was afraid she was going to do something bad. Well, I got her to the doctor and he gave her some medication.

"You have to remember that this is back in the days when things like post-natal depression were sort of new to medical experts. A lot of mental illnesses really. Your mum was afraid they would lock her up, so for the doc to give her some medication instead was kind of radical. But it worked. She was her old self again in no time."

That wasn't necessarily true, I thought. Depression had always been around, but in the past it had been labelled as something else.

"I didn't know," I said.

He nodded. "I know. It was rough for both of us for a while, but what I'm saying is, I know how hard it was for you, trying to help Callie. It can be draining, having someone you love go through such an illness. But you're strong honey. Don't ever forget that."

My grandfather came in later that afternoon, giving me a hug. Dad made him a cup of tea.

Grandad has always been kind of quiet. Dad had told me that his experience fighting in the war in Europe had changed him, made him a little more introspective. His parents, like many Maori of their generation, had struggled to find work in the city. I wished I could say there wasn't such thing as prejudice, but back in the days of the Depression, they faced a lot of it, especially from men who were also struggling to find work and feed their families. It was one of the reasons my great-grandparents decided to move to rural Waikato.

When Grandad came back from the war, three years after enlisting, he opted to stay rather than try to find work again in the city. He often said he liked the peace and quiet of the farm. I think partly he wanted to avoid the problems a lot of urban Maori were facing. I'd heard of some who chose to turn their backs on their heritage. Grandad didn't want to do that.

When Mum and I moved to the city, a lot had changed. The government, or rather previous governments, had been trying to right the wrongs of the past and our culture experienced something of a resurgence. Our native language was being taught in schools. Still, with my Mum being, as we called it, Pakeha, I was torn between two cultures.

When I was a child, not long after I'd moved to the city, there had been a girl who came from a similar cultural background. She had asked me why I hung out with Callie. I pretended not to understand, even though I knew very well what she was implying. That I should be friends with 'my own kind'. The problem was, I couldn't turn my back on either. My parents thought it was important for me to know both sides of it.

My dad's family still observed certain traditions, like a tangi when my grandmother died, but they were more or less private things. The main lesson my grandfather took from the war was that things like a difference in skin colour wasn't worth fighting about.

Grandad drank his tea, while my dad busied himself with making dinner. Grandad's face was lined with liver spots dotted here and there. His skin was brown, darker than my own, which was a light tan in winter and a darker tan in summer.

"How you doing, Bub?" he asked. He'd always called me 'Bub', although I never knew why.

"I'm okay, Grandad."

He raised an eyebrow at me, but didn't comment. I knew what that look meant. He didn't believe me for a second. Then again, he went through losing my grandmother to cancer and that was the hardest thing he ever had to deal with. Even fighting in the war, tough as it was, didn't compare, he'd once told me.

"Come," he said, nodding his head to the porch. It was cool, but not cold and the porch was sheltered from the wind. "Let's have a korero."

"Grandad, I don't really need to have a chat," I said, protesting a little.

He shook his head, refusing to take no for an answer. I sighed and glanced at Dad, but he just smiled and gestured for me to follow my grandfather.

"Go on Chook," he said.

I followed the old man outside and sat on the porch swing beside him, watching as Grandad picked up a packet of tobacco and took out a smaller packet of rice paper, along with a pinch of the tobacco. I screwed up my nose.

"You shouldn't smoke, Grandad," I said.

He grinned at me.

"What's it gonna do, Bub? Kill me?" He laughed.

He'd been smoking since the age of fifteen but either it hadn't seemed to affect his health or I was just never told about any health problems. Working on the land probably helped him a lot. He often told me it was all mind over matter, and given how stubborn the old man could be, I could believe it.

I turned my head and looked out over the paddock, watching as a stray cow wandered lazily in the distance. I heard my grandfather strike a match to light his cigarette. I glanced at him as he blew out a puff of smoke and tried not to cough.

"Very sad," he said, "about your friend."

Over the years, his speech had become kind of stilted. Dad had never confirmed it but I was fairly certain Grandad had had a stroke at some point. Maybe even a couple. Not enough to be completely debilitating, but enough to affect his speech at least.

"Your nana, she was special. When she passed, I didn't want to do anything."

"You still miss her."

He nodded and puffed on his cigarette.

"Ay. Every day."

I knew what he was telling me, without having to verbalise it. He'd taken it hard. Hard enough that he'd become depressed. Losing my grandmother was hard on everyone, but she had been the love of his life.

"When does it stop hurting, Grandad?"

"It never does," he said. "It fades, but it's still there. Always there."

"Everyone keeps telling me to let go."

"You have to, Bub. Remember her, but let her go."

"I don't know if I can. I hate it, but ..." I was quiet

for a moment, not wanting to voice the source of my pain.

"Not your fault, Bub," he said. "You were her friend."

"I wasn't there for her when she needed me."

"Sometimes nothing you can do," he said. "Think I don't wish the same for your nan?"

I knew what he was saying. He'd prayed, sought help from a local elder, asked doctor after doctor, but in the end it had all been for naught.

It didn't stop me feeling guilty. Even though I knew that I had done the best I could, part of me still felt like I hadn't done enough. Another part of me knew that there was something else which had caused this. Callie hadn't asked for help, either out of pride or some other, as yet unknown reason.

That was why I had to keep reading her journals. I was sure she would tell me eventually.

CHAPTER FIFTEEN

Over the next couple of days, I helped my dad and grandad on the farm. The work was hard, but I found a sort of peace in it.

I recalled some of the times Callie would come to the farm. The first summer, we'd gone for a walk in the early morning. I'd told her that if we were quiet enough, we might catch a glimpse of some of the native wildlife. Not any kiwis though, since most of the birds had died out around these parts.

"Why do you like this place so much?" Callie asked me, squinting at the strong rays of the early sun.

"It's peaceful. I can sit on the grass and just listen to the cicadas in the trees."

She shuddered. Callie had never liked what she called 'creepy crawlies'. She had once seen a spider in the classroom at school and had screamed and run out. It had only been a little jumping spider but she had once told me she had a phobia.

As we sat on the grass in the shade of some trees, I could hear the birds calling. Especially the Tui. There were always starlings and sparrows around, but the

Tui was special.

"What's so special about the Tui?" Callie asked.

"Well, legend has it that it's one of the offspring of the Earth Mother and Sky Father."

Callie nodded. She'd always found the Maori legends fascinating. The one thing that had never changed about my culture was the oral traditions which had been passed down for generations.

"When I was a kid we went to Mount Bruce," she told me. "They had a Tui there which liked to wolf whistle at people."

I laughed. Mount Bruce was a wildlife sanctuary in the lower part of the North Island. I'd been once, but it was a long time ago. I didn't remember the Tui, but had heard about it.

We listened for a little while to the birdsong. Callie tilted her head, lifting her face to the sun. I could see her pale skin respond to the sunlight, almost as if it had begun to glow. Callie had always been a morning person. I had become a little lazy. As a teenager I found it difficult getting up in time to go to school, but Callie always liked it. As she got older and the illness took hold, getting out of bed was harder.

"You're right," she said softly. "It is beautiful here."

She seemed so at peace on those mornings.

I woke up early on Wednesday morning. Dad was probably already out, milking the cows, but he wasn't expecting me to come out and help him. I poured some water in the electric kettle and switched it on, waiting for the water to boil. I grabbed a cup and spooned some instant coffee powder into the cup. No coffee makers here, I thought.

Yawning, I made myself a coffee and went out to the porch to sit and enjoy the sunrise. It was cool, but not too cold. A light mist had covered the ground, creating almost ghostly lines through the long grass. The sun was just peeking over the horizon, sending out rays of gold over the misty paddocks, changing the colour of the green grass.

I remembered a poem I read years ago. I'd been introduced to it through a novel I'd read.

Nature's first green is gold
Her hardest hue to hold

I'd forgotten most of the lines, but those first two had stayed with me, It reminded me of the early mornings on the farm, when the sun was just barely up, the grass in the paddocks turning almost golden. The effect was always temporary as the sun slowly rose and the light changed.

"Up early, Bub?"

I turned my head to the door. Grandad stood on the threshold, squinting his eyes at the sun.

"Yeah Grandad. I'm heading up to Auckland today."

"Auckland? What's there, Bub?"

I didn't want to tell my grandfather about the man I was going to stay with. Not that I thought he would judge me for going to stay with a man I barely knew. I felt I was old enough, at thirty-five, to judge the situation for myself. Tom's invitation hadn't implied anything beyond just a place to stay for a few days.

Still, in many ways, my grandfather saw me as the little girl who used to sit on his lap and listen to him when he sang. Music was a very big part of our family, although Grandad doesn't sing much anymore. He used to tell me Nana was the one who had the musical talent in the family.

I heard the cry of the Tui in the trees. I'd been here three days and this was the first morning I'd heard Tui song.

"Sounds like Charlie's back," Grandad observed.

"How do you know that's Charlie?" I asked, remembering the Tui we had nicknamed years ago. Then again, they were all named Charlie.

Grandad winked at me and sat down, rolling himself a cigarette before lighting it.

"You really shouldn't smoke Grandad," I told him, pretending to scold. He just looked at me, not saying a word. He wasn't going to change, but then why should he?

I sat quietly, watching as the mist was slowly burned away.

"Gonna be a good day, ay?" Grandad said.

I nodded. "A good day," I agreed.

I continued to sip my coffee, thinking about the long drive ahead. I was looking forward to seeing Tom. I again felt that tiny fluttering in my stomach as I remembered him at the funeral. It wasn't just that he was good-looking. There had been something about him, something so inherently good that I couldn't help but be attracted to him. I hadn't felt like that about anyone for a very long time.

I finished my coffee and stood up, stretching.

"I should go pack," I said.

"You wanting to get on the road early, Bub?" Grandad asked.

I nodded. I had at least a two-and-a-half-hour drive ahead of me, maybe longer if traffic was bad. I'd heard that it could be particularly bad on the Auckland motorway and as much as I wanted to avoid that, I knew it wasn't going to be easy.

Dad came in as I was preparing breakfast. He usually liked eggs for breakfast. Scrambled, poached, boiled, whatever was easiest. We used to have chickens in the yard and it was my job when I was home to get the eggs. I smiled, thinking of the first time Callie had gone out with me to get the eggs. One of the hens was sitting on an egg and not realising Callie didn't know much about chickens, I asked her to grab it.

"Ow!" she said. "It bit me."

"The egg?"

"No, dummy! The chicken."

"Oh! Yeah, they do that. Sorry."

She sent me a wounded look, rubbing at the spot on her hand where she'd been nipped. It only looked bruised. The skin wasn't even broken.

"You could have warned me," she said petulantly.

"I forgot," I said with a shrug.

Yeah right, was the look she shot me. I had to retrieve the egg myself since Callie didn't trust the hen not to bite her again. I just shooed it away and grabbed the egg.

"What's that smile for, Chook?" Dad asked as I began spooning eggs onto each plate.

"Just thinking about the first time Callie and I went out to get eggs in the chicken coop. The hen bit her."

Dad laughed. "Bet you were popular."

I grinned at him. "She didn't quite trust me after

that." Not in the chicken coop anyway.

We sat down at the table. Grandad took his plate and murmured a prayer in Maori. He always maintained we should offer our thanks for the food. I murmured an 'amen' once he was done.

"Want some toast, Grandad?" I asked, passing him the toast rack.

"Ae. Tena koe, Bub."

Dad ate his eggs slowly, looking thoughtful.

"Something wrong, Dad?" I asked.

"No, Chook. This is good."

We ate in silence for a little. Dad sipped his tea.

"This friend you're going to stay with," he began, looking at me.

"Tom." I had told my dad about him, but only because he had overheard a phone conversation between Tom and I the night I arrived. I'd been reluctant to tell him but my father had always been good at wheedling the truth from me.

He would have been great as an interrogator, I often thought. All he'd have to do is thrust out his lower lip and widen those brown eyes of his and they'd cave. Mum told me that was how he used to manage to win any argument when they were married.

"How much do you know about this man?" he asked.

"We've talked on the phone a lot," I said.

"That doesn't mean much, honey."

"Dad, I'm a grown woman."

He pointed his fork at me. "You still need to be careful."

"Ay Bub," Grandad said. "Never know what's out

there.”

“I don’t think he’s an axe murderer, Grandad.”

My grandfather’s face creased in a deep frown. He clearly didn’t like the implications. Despite my not telling Grandad about Tom, Dad had clearly talked it over with him.

“We’re just concerned,” Dad said. “You barely know this man.”

“And I’m not a child. If the situation looks bad, I can get out of it.”

Dad didn’t seem to like my confidence. He had never really said anything but I sometimes got the impression he didn’t like me being in the city. Not that Napier was all that bad. We did have our share of crime but I was confidence I was smart enough to know what to do if something did happen.

I could understand their concern. I’d only met Tom once, and just because he had told me some things over the phone, it didn’t mean he was a genuine person. Still, I had to trust my instincts that he was exactly what he said he was.

“Dad,” I said quietly, “I know you’re concerned, but I have to trust that he’s okay. Sometimes you just have to trust your instincts.”

“I still don’t like it. He lives in the big smoke.”

“That doesn’t make him a bad person, Dad. Look, would it help if I called you every night?”

“It would,” he said, smiling. He reached over and wrapped an arm around me, kissing me on the temple. “Forgive your old man, sweetheart. Sometimes it’s hard for me to remember that you’re not my little girl anymore.”

"I'll always be your little girl, Dad, just not a child."

He got up, taking the plates and put them in the sink.

"I can do the dishes before I go, Dad," I said. "I know you've got work to do."

Grandad nodded. "Got to finish clearing out the back paddocks."

I thought Grandad was too old to be out working, but stayed wisely silent on the matter. He seemed fit and healthy for a man his age, so who was I to tell him he couldn't do something?

Grandad left to work in the back paddock, but gave me a hug before he did so. I found his arms comforting, taking in the scent of tobacco and that outdoorsy smell that reminded me so much of the times I would go to him for comfort when I hurt myself out playing or working in the field.

Dad waited to see me off. We hadn't talked much about Callie's death beyond that first day. It wasn't that I didn't want to. It just hadn't felt right.

He leaned in through the open window of the car.

"All right?" he asked.

"I'm all right."

"Janet, I know this has been hard on you. It probably sounds like a cliché, but Callie … she's in a better place now. Maybe you need to leave her be. Let her be at peace."

"I know Dad, but I don't think I can be at peace until I understand."

"She loved you, Janet. But sometimes, no matter what we do or how we feel, it isn't enough. It's not your fault. It's not her fault either."

"It still hurts," I said. My voice sounded so small. My dad looked at me in sympathy.

"You have to let her go," he said.

"I'm trying, Dad," I replied. "I'm trying."

"I love you, Bub."

"I love you too, Dad. Tell Grandad ..."

He grinned. "He knows. You know he's not much for goodbyes."

"Yeah, I know. Tell him I love him anyway."

CHAPTER SIXTEEN

As I drove north, I found myself thinking about some of the things I'd read in Callie's journals the few days I was in Te Kuiti. In some of the entries Callie had been talking about finishing school. She had been in what would have been her second to last year of high school, but her dad didn't see the point in her continuing. She had talked about moving away. Trying to find a job in a bigger city.

She had considered moving to Hamilton. While the city was not as big as Auckland, it was growing. Given how high Auckland property prices were, a lot of people were now buying homes in Hamilton and commuting to Auckland, or getting jobs in the smaller city. Of course, when Callie was seventeen, it was still considered very much a provincial city, but unlike Napier, there was a little more room to grow.

Hamilton was now about the fourth biggest city in New Zealand, a little more than one hundred and twenty kilometres from Auckland, and about an hour's drive from my hometown. I had travelled through the city a few times as a teenager, especially when I'd gone to the farm in early winter to help my dad through Field Days, which is an annual event for farmers, hosted just south of Hamilton.

Dad liked to check out the event for the latest innovations in farming machinery and technology. Anything to make it easier for him to do his job, since he didn't really have that many farmhands to help him out anymore. I often wondered what he was going to do when Grandad was gone – perish the thought. It wasn't that I had no interest in the farm, but I couldn't run it by myself either.

As I reached the outskirts of Hamilton, I thought back to those last years of high school with more than a little sadness. I had gone on to my final year of school while Callie had left and tried to get a job. Her father had told her he didn't want her moving away and she was constantly complaining in her journal that he never seemed to want to let her do anything.

Finding a job in Napier, especially when she had no qualifications, had been a tough proposition. She was competing with at least a hundred other people with more experience and qualifications than she had.

After I finished school, I stayed on the farm for a couple of months before I started studying for my diploma at Waikato University. Since I was only going to be there for a year, Dad had wondered why I didn't choose to stay on the farm and attend my classes, but even with the small car he'd bought me when I finished high school, it was too long a commute.

I boarded with a couple of women who were friends of a friend of my dad's. They were a gay couple, but it wasn't something they flaunted and it never really mattered to me. While I felt my grandad was a little perturbed by it, he never said anything. My dad had met them and wasn't at all worried. He had probably been glad someone would be looking after me.

After I'd been there a couple of months, Callie called and told me she had found a job in a supermarket. In Hamilton. So she was moving in to a flat with two others, both of whom were students. I wondered if part of the reason she had decided to try for the job was because I was there. We had missed each other terribly.

I had a week off studying so I went to Napier to help her pack her things. The flat was furnished, so she only needed her clothes and her own linen. She was still living with her parents. She hadn't been able to get a job for over a year and was on the unemployment benefit, but because of various restrictions, she wasn't able to get much and most of what she did get paid was given to her parents to help with expenses.

I had offered to take her in my car, as she couldn't afford a car of her own. We hadn't seen each other in months and had spent most of the week just catching up, talking about anything and everything.

She seemed nervous as I helped her pack a suitcase. I wondered if she was worried about moving so far away.

"You okay?" I asked.

"Yeah," she replied. "Just, you know, it's a big change."

While Callie had lived most of her life in Napier, it was still a smaller city than Hamilton, or Auckland for that matter, and she wasn't used to being so far away from home.

But that was then and I now had the benefit of hindsight. I had read in her journal that Callie had been diagnosed with clinical depression, but even then it hadn't been a subject people talked openly about it. I had read with dismay that she had thought the diagnosis of mental illness meant she was crazy.

When I thought back to that afternoon, it wasn't just nervousness I'd sensed. She had been pale, or paler than normal, with dark circles under her eyes, yet I knew from what her mother had told me at the time, she had been sleeping a lot.

"So are these people nice? The ones you're moving in with?"

She shrugged. "I guess."

"What about the supermarket?"

"It's a job," she said, sighing. She seemed resigned.

"You could always enrol in a course or something," I suggested gently. "If you don't like the supermarket. The university has one-year diplomas."

"Dad doesn't want me getting in debt."

I frowned. "Well, how much would it be?"

"More money than I have," she said with a sigh.

It always used to bother me that she didn't seem to have the courage to say what she really wanted. I knew she wanted to do some kind of course. She had loved anything to do with woodworking at school, but Richard had always told her it wasn't the right kind of environment for her.

At times I felt her father was a bit of a chauvinist, but I realised after the long talk we'd had a few days ago that he was trying to protect her from disappointment. Women trying to find work in a field that had always been considered a 'male profession' often had to work twice as hard to prove themselves. Callie could work hard at something she really wanted, but I realised he never thought she was strong enough emotionally to put up with the teasing and jibes that would come with working in that field.

It was too bad that he never trusted Callie enough to know what she wanted.

It annoyed me that he had discouraged her from doing something she loved that much, and that he'd decided what he thought she could handle. Maybe Callie would have been happier for it, and maybe she would have proven him wrong. It was a lot of maybes, and it had never been tested.

I knew Callie had looked up to her father, but he was nowhere near perfect. After all, this was a man who never really achieved much in his life, according to him.

I wondered if he was jealous because Callie was smarter than him.

I drove through the main street of Hamilton on my way north, passing the supermarket she had worked at. I had been so busy studying that I didn't really spend a lot of time socialising. The university campus was on the eastern side of Hamilton and a few kilometres from the inner city.

Still, Callie and I had always made time to see each other at least once a month, going out to movies or to lunch at a small café. Callie never talked much about her illness and me being so absorbed in my studies, I probably didn't realise she was sick. Not then, at least.

It was getting close to lunchtime when I made it to the Mercer area. Mercer was pretty much a village at the southern-most point of Auckland. There wasn't much to see. Just rolling hills and what some people would call a truck stop, with a service station and a café. It was off the main highway so people on long drives could turn off and take a break if they need to. There are always billboards on the highway telling people to take a break if they were tired, which I always thought was a good idea.

I decided to stop in at the cafe and get a coffee. They had some muffins which looked delicious and fresh so I bought one of those as well and sat down at a table in the corner. They had furnished the café with comfortable armchairs where people could sit back and relax and I had brought in Callie's journal.

The girl on the counter brought out my cappuccino and I looked up from the journal, giving her a brief smile of thanks before shifting in my seat to grab a couple of packets of sugar. The cups they used in cafes were not nearly the same size as the coffee mugs I used at home so I tended to take a lot less sugar.

I sweetened my coffee and stirred it, then sat back again and began reading.

Janet and I had lunch at McD's today. She was talking about this psychology class she was taking. She really seems to be enjoying studying. I wish I could go to uni but it's so expensive and I'm not getting much at the supermarket.

I hate my job. I hate the customers. Okay, some of them are nice, but there was this one lady. She kept arguing about the prices of things, saying our signs were 'misleading' and she was going to tell Consumer Complaints all about our bad business practices, making it sound like we were trying to con her.

I rolled my eyes at that. Consumer Complaints was a programme on television that had been on since before Callie and I were born where people who felt they had been ripped off or scammed wrote in and the stories were investigated. It was a good show and they did stand up for the little guy, but I very much doubted they would have listened to some woman complaining about supermarket prices. From what I knew of the place Callie worked in, it was supposed to be the cheapest in town.

Then there was this big guy who was like way taller than me and he was very angry looking. I guess he liked intimidating girls or something because even though there was a counter between us it felt like he was standing over me. He claimed I had given him the wrong change, even though I know I hadn't because it was all there on the computer. My manager came over and asked what the problem was and he spoke to her in just as snotty a tone saying I had given him the wrong change, like I'd given him a ten instead of a twenty. She just opened the till and gave him twenty dollars and he looked so smug. When they counted down my till later, they found it was short, by exactly twenty dollars. Well, guess who ends up having to pay it back? I hate scammers.

I don't tell Janet any of this. She doesn't need to know about my horrible job. She's so happy with everything she's learning and all her new friends at uni. She doesn't need to know about my problems.

I had to go see the doctor today. He wants me to go see

someone and he put me on anti-depressants. I hate that stuff. It always makes me feel like a zombie. I know Janet's noticed I'm tired all the time, but I don't want to tell her about this either. It's bad enough that my parents think I'm just being stupid. They don't believe that it's a real illness and just tell me to get over it. The one person I did tell told me the same thing.

I remembered asking her that day if things were okay and she'd just dismissed it, saying everything was fine. I sat there in that chair, my heart breaking for my friend, clearly worried that I would be just as dismissive of her illness. I had known from my psychology papers that it was a real thing and telling someone in that situation to 'get over it' was the worst possible thing anyone could do.

Hindsight was always twenty-twenty, but if I had known then what I knew now ... As much as it hurt, since she died, I keep asking myself the same questions. Would she be alive now if I had known then just how bad things were? Had I been so self-involved that I had never seen how troubled she was?

It took five years for me to learn Callie was sick. Looking back now, there had always been signs, which I had somehow missed. I'd put it down to stress, never thinking it could be something far more serious.

CHAPTER SEVENTEEN

I had thought about calling in to see Susan on my way to Tom's place, but we had barely spoken since the funeral. I did call her a couple of times but I always got the feeling she wanted nothing to do with me now that Callie was gone. To give her credit, it couldn't have been an easy thing for her, finding her dying flatmate. Still, I had thought she would have at least wanted to talk about it. Then again, she and Callie had had a few blow-ups from time to time.

One day Callie and I had been talking on the phone and she had rudely barged into Callie's room.

"Can you hurry up?" she said, sounding in a bad mood. "I need to use the phone."

Callie had sounded annoyed as she spoke to her flatmate.

"I'm on the phone with Janet."

"You've been on the phone for hours," Susan complained. "I want to call my boyfriend."

That had been a gross exaggeration, since we'd barely been on ten minutes. Callie later told me Susan had always grumbled about the expensive phone bills and wanted to cancel it, but she was also always the one using the phone and calling friends all over the country, so she was complaining about something of her own making. Callie never said anything to Susan, however, I supposed for the sake of peace. Finding good flats for a reasonable rent was difficult enough.

She did the same when we were talking on Skype, interrupting our conversation as if what she had to say was more important than Callie talking to me. I didn't want to say Susan was selfish, or self-involved, but it did feel that way sometimes.

Callie had been talking about her job when Susan had yet again barged in and interrupted.

"When are you gonna give me the money for the tv?" she asked.

Callie had frowned at her.

"What money?"

"You're supposed to pay for half the tv," Susan said, rolling her eyes.

"You mean the tv that I never get to watch?" Callie replied, glancing at the screen with a look of discomfort.

"That's not my problem," Susan snapped. "I need that money!"

She'd walked out of the room without so much as an apology for being so rude. I looked at Callie.

"She expects you to pay half for a tv you don't even watch?"

Callie shrugged. "We're supposed to pay half the expenses."

"Expenses. Like phone and power," I pointed out. "Not new appliances, especially when you're not sharing them. That's not fair, Callie."

"I can't tell her that," my friend said with a sigh.

I didn't pursue it, but I could tell Callie was not happy with the situation. She had told me she wasn't getting paid as much as Susan and she didn't have much cash to spare at the end of the pay period.

There had been times I would get the feeling that Susan barely noticed Callie. Then again, Callie did have a habit of trying to disappear into the woodwork, so to speak.

If I was honest with myself, the main reason I didn't want to call in on Susan was because in part I blamed her for what happened to Callie. Like if she had been a better friend, Callie might not have done what she did. It sounded harsh, even in my mind, but it was just how I felt.

I drove on to Tom's place without detouring to the flat. Tom lived on the western side of Auckland city in a suburb which overlooked the harbour. It was pretty, although I still preferred Napier.

His house was about a half hour drive through the suburbs, or about twenty minutes on the motorway, if the traffic was clear. It was only about two in the afternoon, so it wasn't too bad. I still wasn't confident enough to drive all the way on that motorway.

Tom told me he had bought the house from his parents, who had decided to buy a smaller place not far from his own. He also told me that he had asked Callie's friend, Miranda, to move into his second bedroom. She had been staying with another friend of Callie's, but after Callie died, the friend had got a job in another town. Miranda didn't want to leave.

He had felt sorry for the young girl, who, now that her mother was gone, as well as Callie, didn't have anyone. Her father had tried to get custody when he found out her mother was terminally ill, but thanks to a sympathetic social worker, she had successfully applied to be considered an independent minor. That had apparently been Callie's suggestion.

I was again reminded of Callie's habit of picking up strays. She had been the same most of her life.

In high school, there had been a girl a couple of years behind us who had been even shyer than Callie. The girl had also been a victim of the bullying that went on and Callie had taken her under her wing.

I'd read stories about people in similar situations to Callie who stood up for others like themselves, but found it so difficult when it came to their own lives. Was that what she was doing with Miranda, I wondered. Had she seen something in the teenage girl that was so like her own problems? Why was it easier for her to try to fix someone else's issues, but so hard to fix her own?

Why had Callie never been able to stand up for herself? With her flatmate? With her dad?

I guessed that no matter how bad things were, she just didn't have the strength to do so. She'd often said that it tended to be a lot harder to stand up to the people you love than it was to stand up to strangers. I was reminded of a movie we had seen together. It was supposedly a kids' movie, one of a series, but the later ones seemed to be darker in tone and less appropriate for children. In the movie, one of the characters had stood up to his friends, and another character had said pretty much the same thing. That it was easier to stand up to an enemy than it was a friend.

As I drove up the street looking for the house, I was conscious of another car following behind. The driver appeared to be a little impatient, getting too close to my own car. He didn't seem to understand that I was looking for an address. Either that or he just didn't care. I sighed, thinking people were so impatient nowadays. It was one of the reasons I didn't like the big cities. Home just seemed to be so much quieter. So much more laidback.

I slowed down and indicated I was going to move to the side of the road to let him pass while I looked around for the number. He eyed me as he passed, a huge scowl on his face. I sent him an apologetic smile which seemed to throw him. He drove on but in that brief moment I thought I saw a little answering smile on his lips.

I continued on down the road, locating the letterbox which stood outside Tom's home. He had a one-level brown brick home that was probably about twenty years old. It looked neat and tidy, the front lawn was short and a lush green, the trimmings on the house clean and sparkling as if they had been freshly painted. The aluminium framed windows reflected the blue sky, the light dancing off the glass.

There was a car parked in the driveway. A late model Ford Mondeo. I laughed, thinking of the so-called rivalry between Holden owners and Ford owners. It apparently dated back a few decades or so in Australia and centred around motorsports, specifically Bathurst. Every year they held some kind of endurance race in the Australian city and both makes had featured prominently.

My father had owned Holden vehicles for years, so it was natural for me, when it came to buying a new car, to choose a model from the same 'family'.

As I parked my Barina next to the Mondeo, I noticed Tom grinning at me from the front porch. I got out of the car and he approached. I felt that slight shiver I always seemed to get when I thought about him. He was even more gorgeous than I remembered. The man could have been a model; he was that good-looking.

Then again, maybe I'm just biased or something, I thought.

"Okay, this will never do," he joked, chuckling. "You cannot own a Holden. It's not allowed."

Cheeky bugger, I thought, deciding to give it right back to him.

"Yeah? "So who went and made you the boss of me?"

He laughed, wrapping his arms around me in a huge hug. I went into his arms easily, taking in the scent of his aftershave. It was a woodsy scent, reminding me a little of the farm. It sounds silly, but he did smell clean and fresh, and wonderful.

"I'm glad you're here, Janet," he said softly.

"Me too," I replied.

He walked me inside, telling me we could get my stuff later. There was a small hallway leading to an open-plan living room, kitchen and dining area. The kitchen bench, or counter had three sides. Two were against the wall which looked out onto the yard. A breakfast bar was on the other side of the third side, separating the kitchen from the dining part. The kitchen was fairly large.

"You want a tour of the house or would you like a coffee first?"

"Ooh, tough choice. Coffee," I said, and he laughed again. He had a nice, deep laugh, his brown eyes sparkling with amusement.

I stood beside the counter, watching as Tom filled the kettle with water from the tap and put it on to boil. He bustled around the kitchen, grabbing mugs from a little mug tree beside the sink and spooning freeze-dried coffee into each mug before adding sugar and milk to mine. As he began to put in the third teaspoonful he shot me a look. I looked back at him, knowing he was about to say something teasing. He thought it was hilarious that I had such a sweet tooth.

The kettle boiling saved him from a sarcastic retort and he busied himself with making the coffee. He picked up the mugs and carried them around to the table, placing one mug on a coaster to protect the polished dark brown veneer of the table top. He clearly liked keeping things neat and clean, which was a lot better than I was. Not that I was a slob by any means.

I grinned at him as he pulled out a chair, obviously for me, and we sat down.

"So how did your visit with your dad go?"

"It went fine," I said. "Dad worries."

"Yeah, they do that. My mum's like that with me. Even though they just live down the road a bit she still calls me first thing in the morning and last thing at night."

He sent me a look of exasperation, then laughed. He was very close to his parents, so I knew he didn't really mind.

I nodded. "Dad kept asking about you. Maybe he thought you were an axe murderer or something," I added with a cheesy grin.

He laughed, then sobered. "How do you know I'm not?" he said in an ominous voice.

I nearly choked on my coffee as he said that. Then he broke out in a wide grin. I punched his shoulder.

"Shut up! Idiot!"

"Sorry, but you did walk right into that one."

"Did not," I replied.

"Did too," he said, sipping his coffee and averting his eyes, but not before I saw them crinkling at the corners. He was laughing at me.

"Well, anyway, Dad's not a big fan of the city," I said. "Guess he's afraid I'll be attacked or something."

Tom smiled at me. "Don't worry. I'll protect you. I have a black belt."

I glanced down at the jeans he was wearing. Tom had been a big fan of a karate movie from the eighties, although he'd never taken a single class in karate. I just remembered a quote from the movie which he had got a kick out of.

The main character had asked his teacher what kind of belt he had, meaning what grade of karate he was. The teacher had shown him a leather belt and said he'd bought it from a local store for a good price.

Tom laughed at me, knowing I was remembering that line.

"Joke," he said.

"I knew that," I replied quickly, making him laugh harder.

There it was again, that little tingle I felt when he laughed. His friends often told him he had a weird sense of humour, but I liked it. He reminded me a little of Callie, who had laughed at the same jokes.

He must have seen my expression change as the image of my best friend came to mind. He squeezed my hand gently.

"Hey, Callie wouldn't want you to be sad," he said.

"I know," I replied softly. "It's just ... I get reminded of something she did or something she liked and it just hurts to know that she's not here." I didn't want to get maudlin, but I couldn't help it. Still, I thought he understood, more than even my friends did.

"It's been really bad at work," he said with a heavy sigh. "Phil's been a real bastard with the woman they hired to replace Callie. They had to get in a temp and he didn't want to train her. I overheard her talking to Kat the other day, wondering why Phil was being so horrible to her. She was shocked when Kat told her what had happened."

"I can't imagine how tough it must be for someone to come in like that, not knowing why, and for Callie's ex-boss to act like that." I frowned. It seemed as if Phil's reaction was a little extreme for someone they thought hadn't liked Callie or had treated her as badly as he did.

Tom sighed, running a hand through his hair, which was a little long and flopped over his forehead.

"I really don't get the guy. I mean, he acts like he can boss everyone around, talks down to his colleagues and is making everyone else on his team miserable."

"Do you think there might have been something else going on?" I asked.

Tom shrugged. "Who knows?"

The front door slammed and Miranda came in. Her eyes widened as she saw me.

"Hi," she said shyly.

"Hi Miranda."

She was wearing jeans and a sweatshirt and carrying a backpack which looked heavy.

"How was school?" Tom asked as she put the backpack down beside the door and went into the kitchen. I watched as she grabbed a glass from the cupboard and a bottle of juice from the fridge, pouring herself some.

She had put on a little weight since I'd seen her. Not much, but just enough so she didn't look so unhealthy.

"It was okay. I've got so much catching up to do, but the teachers are really cool."

"You went back to school?" I asked, remembering a conversation I'd had not so long ago with Tom, who had been trying to talk her into going back.

She nodded, sipping her juice. "Callie and me used to talk about school a lot. I mean, Callie and I," she corrected, making a face. Then she seemed to realise. "Sorry, I ..."

"It's okay," I said. "It's good to talk about her."

"She told me once she regretted leaving school when she did. She said education was important. My mum was like that too. Callie said she didn't want me to miss out on my dreams."

There again was that feeling that Callie was a 'do as

I say, not as I do' kind of person. I just couldn't see why it was so hard for her to pursue the things she wanted. I was so sure there was something I wasn't seeing. I once again found myself hoping the journals would have the answer.

"So, how long are you staying Janet?" Miranda asked.

"A few days. That's if you guys can put up with me that long," I added, rolling my eyes for effect.

Miranda giggled.

"You're funny," she said. "That's why Callie liked you, you know. You could always make her laugh."

"Well, that's my job," I replied.

She giggled again.

"We're going to the basketball tonight," Tom said. "Wanna come?"

"I can't. I have heaps of homework to do and then I have to work at the restaurant."

"What time do you finish?" he asked her. "Janet and I can pick you up."

She looked at him, clearly about to turn him down, but I smiled at her kindly.

"If it's no trouble," she said.

"Whatchu talkin' about?" he replied, putting on what sounded like a bad imitation of an accent from someone from somewhere in New York. "Ain't no trouble."

Miranda giggled again, then picked up her bag.

"Okay. I finish at ten thirty."

"Great. We'll be waiting outside."

Miranda's smile could have lit up the room. She walked out to her room, leaving us alone once more.

CHAPTER EIGHTEEN

Since the basketball game was starting around seven, Tom decided we could have an early dinner. Miranda had told him she would grab a salad at work, since she was given a meal allowance if she was working more than four hours. It wasn't the healthiest of meals, but Miranda was philosophical about it.

Tom had helped me get my stuff out of the car, taking my little case. I had packed reasonably light, not sure how long I would be staying. Tom sent me an odd look. I guessed he thought I would be one to pack everything but the kitchen sink, but that just wasn't me.

The house had three bedrooms. One was obviously the master bedroom with its own bathroom. Miranda had taken the second largest bedroom, while the spare bedroom was just big enough for a double bed and a small chest of drawers. I didn't mind the size, since I wasn't planning on staying for longer than ten days. I didn't want to impose.

Tom had seen the box of journals I had brought in but hadn't made a comment. I knew what it looked like. There were at least thirty notebooks in the box and I'd already been through twenty. Callie had written a lot in those early years.

Once I had unpacked, I went back out to the kitchen where Tom was preparing dinner.

"What are you making?" I asked.

"I thought I'd make Chicken Alfredo with a salad."

"Mm, sounds good," I said, watching as he began slicing the chicken into strips and seasoned it before placing it in a hot pan. He worked with confidence.

"So, where did you learn to cook?" I asked, observing the ease with which he cut up the ingredients. I tended to chop haphazardly while Tom appeared more like a professional chef.

"My parents. They own their own restaurant in town, although Dad doesn't cook much there anymore." He grinned at me. "Mum swore black and blue that no child of hers was going to grow up not knowing how to cook."

I grinned. They sounded like great people.

"How did your parents meet?"

"They were both taking a hospitality course. Mum's was more on the administrative side while Dad went on to major in the culinary arts. He's won a few awards for his dishes, although he still says he's no Andy Lo Bianco."

I snorted. Andrew Lo Bianco, an American chef whose family on his father's side owned a chain of restaurants in Italy, had a reputation for having a bad temper on a tv show he had once appeared on, although apparently from what I read he was nothing like that when he was around kids or his family.

Despite that, he was an excellent cook from what I saw.

"Of course not," I replied. "I doubt he swears at his staff like Lo Bianco does."

Tom chuckled. "You're right. He doesn't." He continued to chat as he worked, telling me about growing up with his two brothers, one older and one younger and his sister, who was the baby of the family. He related some funny incidents all around being the middle son.

I envied him in many ways, having grown up with three siblings. Not that I minded having been an only child, but still, it would have been nice to have had someone to play with on the farm.

"So, how did you and Callie meet?" he asked.

I told him about my parents' divorce and my mother moving to Napier, then meeting Callie at school and growing up together. Some of it I'd already told him, but he still listened, nodding now and then, giving the odd chuckle.

He told me he had met Callie when he'd been hired on as an accountant at the company about eighteen months earlier. She had been sitting alone in the building's café, reading a book. He'd recognised the name of the author and had asked her about it. They'd ended up having a deep discussion about the merits of certain writers. He'd found Callie to be highly intelligent and he'd enjoyed talking with her so much that the next time they'd met over their lunch break he'd gone armed with knowledge, hoping to draw her into another debate.

He'd often wondered the same thing I did. For

someone so intelligent, why did Callie struggle so much? Why was she stuck in the same job year after year, never given the chance to advance?

Dinner was delicious. The alfredo sauce was cheesy and creamy. The salad was crisp, with a dressing that had just the right bite to it. Tom had told me that cooking was only part of it. A cook had to know how to pick the freshest ingredients as well. Judging from the dinner he'd served up, he knew what he was talking about.

We left for the stadium half an hour later. While I was hardly athletic, the one sport I did enjoy watching was basketball. It was one of the few games that I understood the rules to. I didn't always get the chance to see the games at home, but when I did, I always went to the stadium. It just seemed like a different atmosphere than watching it on television.

Tom bought us drinks and we took our seats, watching the pre-game entertainment.

"Hey, Tommy!"

I looked around at the red-haired man standing beside me and frowned. I recognised his face, but couldn't quite place him. He was a good-looking man with a friendly smile and kind, green eyes, but he made me feel very self-conscious with the way he was gazing at me.

"Hey Jake," Tom said with a smile. "This is Janet. She's staying with me for a few days. Janet, this doofus is my best friend and neighbour, Jake."

Jake smiled back and sat down beside me. "I saw you today, driving up the road. You looked a little lost."

I bit my lip, then remembered. He was the man who had been driving behind me when I'd been looking for Tom's address.

"Oh, hi," I said. "Yeah, I don't know the city that well."

"She's from Napier," Tom added.

"Yeah," Jake laughed. "I guessed you weren't from around here from the way you were crawling down the street. Sorry I got so impatient with you. If I'd known I was following such a beautiful woman, I'd have stopped to help you out."

I found myself blushing. "Um, thanks," I said. I was a little embarrassed by the flirting. It wasn't that I didn't consider myself attractive, but men didn't usually flirt so blatantly with me either.

He grinned. "So, what's a gorgeous girl like you doing with a loser like him?" he asked, nodding at Tom.

"Jake," Tom said warningly. I wondered what that was about, but didn't call him on it. Tom looked at me. "Sorry. Jake tends to run his mouth off sometimes."

"It's fine," I said, smiling at him. Jake didn't need to know the circumstances of how Tom and I had met.

I tried to focus on the show on the court, but Jake continued to flirt with me. It didn't make me uncomfortable as such, but I did think it was a little rude, considering I was there with Tom. Finally, Tom growled another warning and told his friend to back off. As I looked at him, I realised Tom was jealous.

Maybe it was wrong, and not that I had done anything to encourage Jake, but I liked that Tom was jealous. I wondered if he was feeling the same thing I was. Even if it was just an attraction that neither of us were ready to admit to.

The game finally started and we focused on the action on the court. A team from further south, the Manawatu Meerkats, were playing the West Auckland Eagles. What was it with some sports that they named their teams after animals? I thought with a sigh.

The visiting team was actually pretty good. I observed them performing a couple of manoeuvres that elicited cheers from the watching crowd, even those who had been cheering for the home team. One of the Manawatu players, a tall man with the name Johnson emblazoned on his shirt had been bouncing the ball from a position in almost the centre of the court. He feinted and dodged his opponent before practically leaping in the air and shooting a basket, something the average player wouldn't have been able to do.

Tom looked at me as the watching crowd cheered at the move.

"You know why they do that," he explained, unncecessarily. "I mean, that was a pretty slick move on Johnson's part. Just because they're the rival team, doesn't mean the crowd doesn't appreciate the skill."

"I know," I said. "It's one of the things I like about the game."

"Sorry," he replied with a sheepish look. "It probably sounds a little sexist but not many girls, uh, women, sorry, like basketball."

I nudged him. "I'm not most women," I told him.

He gazed at me and for a moment I held my breath. He was so close and I could feel that tingling up my spine again.

"You're not, are you," he said softly.

We were close enough to kiss, and I wanted him to. It was odd. I'd never become so close to someone in such a short time; especially someone I had only met once before, in such terrible circumstances, and talked to over the phone.

I didn't know what it was about him that made me feel so comfortable with him and get butterflies in my stomach at the same time.

A roar went up from the crowd and we turned back to watch as Johnson once again took possession of the ball and ran down the court, passing to another of his teammates for another basket.

The rest of the game passed in a blur. I couldn't stop thinking about Tom and the way he made me feel. I'd had boyfriends, but none of them had made me feel like I had an instant connection with them.

Even Tom's friend Jake seemed to notice the electricity between us. Tom had gone out for a few minutes and Jake looked at me.

"I was beginning to think you two should get a room and get it over with," he said.

I frowned at him.

"What do you mean?" I asked, pretending I didn't know what he was implying. Jake didn't have the chance to elaborate as Tom chose that moment to come back.

I was quiet in the car on the way to pick up Miranda from work, but questions kept running through my mind. Did I really have the courage to pursue this ... whatever it was? Was Tom really attracted to me or was it just because he had had a friendship with Callie?

Miranda seemed to notice the atmosphere between us as well, but didn't say anything. Tom was just as quiet as he followed us inside. He watched Miranda go to her room, scratching his upper lip.

"Uh, well, I should get to bed," he said. "I have to go to work in the morning. Um, feel free to help yourself to anything."

He passed me to go to his room. I bit my lip.

"Tommy," I said, then blushed. "I mean, Tom."

He smiled softly. "I like Tommy," he replied.

"Thanks for tonight. It was nice. I mean, I had a good time."

"So did I," he replied quietly. "I'll see you tomorrow Janet."

"Goodnight."

I couldn't help the grin on my face as I went to my room and closed the door.

I decided to read more of Callie's journal.

I hate working at the supermarket. There's this guy there who always picks on me and makes me do the worst jobs. He's not even a manager. I don't know why he keeps picking on me.

The other day he asked me to go out with him. I couldn't believe it. The guy who picked on me was asking me out on a date. Of course I said no. I don't even like him.

I don't think he liked that very much. He keeps on asking and doesn't want to take no for an answer.

A few days later there was another entry about the man in the supermarket. I remembered this. It was the incident Callie had talked about where he had lied about her to the manager and she'd almost been fired

for it.

I called Janet and she came right over. I know she's got more important things to do. I don't know why she always comes when I call. I hate that I have to call her. I should be able to handle this stuff on my own. It's not fair on her. She's supposed to be studying for exams, not worrying about me.

Oh Callie, I thought, if you only knew that I needed you as much as you needed me. I had never told her how much I depended on her friendship. She was always my sounding board, the one person who encouraged me when I wanted to give up. I had never told her how difficult I found my studies. She had always been better than me at writing essays and it was the one thing I had always hated about studying. I'd always gone to her to help me correct any mistakes in my work, because even though it wasn't her field, she was the smartest person I knew.

How could she have considered herself such a burden when there were many times when I wondered if I was asking too much of her? I knew how much it hurt her that she could never afford to continue her education.

Guilt sat like a hard knot in my stomach. Callie had always had this bad image of herself, but maybe I had contributed by not telling her how much her friendship meant to me.

I turned the light off long after midnight had passed but my sleep was troubled by dreams in which Callie shouted at me, telling me it was my fault. When I woke in the morning, my eyes were wet from the tears I'd shed in my sleep.

CHAPTER NINETEEN

I got up, unable to shake off the dreams. It was almost a relief to find I was alone in the house, Tom having gone to work and Miranda to school. I ate breakfast, wondering what I should do. Part of me wanted to read more of the journal but the other part of me didn't want to read more, still blaming myself for not being there for Callie.

Tom had left me a key and I decided it was a good time to do a little exploring. I dressed in loose pants and a t-shirt and sweatshirt, taking the key and my phone with me in case I needed my map application.

I walked along the street, feeling as if something was weighing me down. I knew it was guilt, but it didn't seem like there was anything I could do to let it go.

I was so lost in thought I didn't see the car until it stopped beside me.

"Janet?" a man's voice called.

I frowned and lifted my head, staring at the man in the car. Jake.

"Uh, hi Jake."

"Sorry, you looked miles away," he said with a

smile. "Is everything okay?"

"Yeah, I'm just, you know, taking a walk. Exploring."

He frowned at me. "It didn't look that way to me," he said. "Look, why don't you come and get a coffee with me."

I shook my head. "Thanks, but I really shouldn't ..."

He bit his lip. "Look, I know I can come across as a bit of a flirt and it can make some girls uncomfortable. I just ... when I saw you, you looked like someone who needed a friendly ear. I promise I'm not an axe murderer," he added with a cheeky grin.

I rolled my eyes at him. "You've been talking to Tom."

He chuckled. "Yeah. So what d'you say? Can I charm you into a cup of coffee with me?"

I gazed at him, wondering if I should trust him. He was Tom's friend and I barely knew him. Then again, I had put an awful lot of trust in Tom as well by staying in his house. In this day and age, it wasn't exactly the smartest thing to do, no matter how long we'd been talking for.

Jake thrust out his bottom lip, attempting a pout and I couldn't help laughing.

"All right," I said. "One coffee."

He smiled. "Great. There's a café just down the road. Hop in."

True to his word, Jake drove to the suburb's shopping centre, only a couple of hundred metres away. He led me to a small café and ordered coffees for both of us, then sat me down in a quiet spot in the corner.

"Maybe it's none of my business," he said, "but I can't help the feeling that there's something going on. Something's upset you."

"I ..." I shook my head, really not knowing what to say in reply.

"Janet, I don't know if Tommy told you, but I have a psych degree. I'm not a psychiatrist, and I don't practice anymore as a counsellor, but I do have some knowledge in this area. Whatever it is that's bothering you, I think you need to talk to someone. At least share some of what you're feeling."

I gazed at him for a long moment.

"He told you, didn't he?" I said flatly. "How we met."

He nodded. "Some of it. Tom came to me for advice, not long after you and he started talking to each other. Janet, maybe I don't know what it's like to lose someone close to me, especially in such circumstances, but maybe that's not the point."

"I keep wondering if there's something I did, or didn't do," I said, sighing.

Our coffees were brought over and I sat back, keeping silent for a moment until the waitress went back to the counter. Jake watched me for a moment as I stirred sugar into my coffee. I wondered if he was waiting for me to say something else, but instead he looked kindly at me.

"You feel guilty. Janet, that's a natural feeling. It's part of the grieving process."

"I know. I've studied psychology."

He studied me for a moment and I realised how

stupid that sounded. One year of psychology papers did not make me an expert on grieving or mental illness for that matter. It was something of a revelation. I'd been spending all these weeks thinking I knew what I was dealing with, and what Callie had been going through, and realised I never really knew at all.

Jake didn't comment on it, to his credit.

"But there's more, isn't there?" he prodded gently.

"Yeah. She left these journals, right from when we were kids. She's always talking about how she kept things from me because she was afraid of being a burden."

"Did you ever tell her she wasn't?"

"How could I? I didn't even know she had these feelings."

"But part of you is wondering if perhaps you should have recognised some sign. That you should have known there was something wrong."

"Well, it's true. I should have."

He looked down as he stirred his coffee, keeping silent for a few minutes, then looked back up at me.

"I have to wonder Janet. Are you more angry at yourself, or at your friend?"

"Myself, I guess. But maybe her as well. A little of both," I admitted, knowing how confusing that probably sounded. He looked like he understood anyway as he smiled gently and nodded. "I mean, Callie was my best friend. Why didn't I see the signs?"

"Some people are more open about their illnesses and some people aren't. I read something that really brought home to me why it's such a hard thing to deal with. For both the sufferer and the people around them."

"What's that?"

"Simply that if a person suffering from depression was actually able to show physical symptoms of it, others wouldn't tell them to 'get over it'. Janet, there is a reason why depression is called an invisible illness, and it's not just because you can't actually see what's going on. It's also because the people around them don't know how to deal with it and don't fully understand it. They try to pretend it doesn't exist. So those like your friend Callie suffer through it alone."

I couldn't help the lump in my throat at the thought of my best friend suffering something so horrible, feeling so alone that suicide was the only way out.

"If she would have told me what she was going through, I would have been there for her," I said.

He nodded in understanding.

"Sadly, even when they have friends or family who are supportive, it isn't quite as easy as all that." He finished his coffee and leaned back. "Do you remember those cartoons on tv where characters have miniature versions of themselves on their shoulders?"

I'd loved cartoons as a child, especially Disney ones. I remembered a couple of scenes of the type he'd talked about.

"Sometimes depression is like those characters. On one shoulder, they have the angel, telling them it'll all be okay and they are not a burden if they talk to someone, even friends and family. On the other shoulder is the devil, telling them they are nothing but a burden and a waste of space. Sometimes one side wins, the other doesn't."

"Do you think that's what happened to Callie?" I asked.

"I don't know, but then, I didn't know your friend and not everyone experiences it the same way. Tom hasn't told me much about her except that they were friends at work and he cared for her."

I bit my lip. "Sometimes when I'm talking to him, I get the impression he wanted more than that. Like he wanted to ask her out."

Jake smiled.

"Tom's an awesome guy. From the way he described her, he could have done worse. But he's always been kind of shy."

"So was Callie," I said.

He groaned, then laughed.

"Both as bad as each other by the sound of it. I doubt you'd have that problem."

"I think that's why Callie and I got along so well," I told him. His smile broadened.

"The whole opposites attract thing? Yeah, I can see that happening." He sobered. "Janet, don't be mad at Tom okay? I know a lot of the things you two have talked about have been in confidence. It's just ... he needed to talk to someone. He's worried about you. This obsession you have for finding out the truth isn't healthy."

"I just need to know. And I'm not mad at him. I understand why he came to you."

"The thing is, I think he likes you. Judging from what I saw last night, it seems to be mutual. It probably sounds strange to you, but Tom hasn't had a lot of girlfriends. Most of the time, he shies away from relationships, thinking the girls are only in it for his looks. He's not shallow by any means."

I'd already got that impression from talking to him. I could understand why he was so reticent. Especially if I'd got into a relationship with someone who was only in it because they had a certain image of me that I couldn't possibly live up to.

"I actually haven't had a lot of relationships either," I admitted.

"Janet, this probably sounds like I'm being a total nosey parker, but why did you come up here? Tom said you live in Napier."

"I do. I …"

I wasn't even sure myself why I'd taken up his offer. Sure, there had been that attraction I felt, but was that really the only reason I had chosen to stay with him? After Alex had decided I needed a short leave of absence, I had wanted to get out of my own headspace and Tom's offer had sounded like just what I needed. But why him? Why hadn't I gone to stay with other friends?

The only other reason I could think of was Callie. He had seen a side of her that I hadn't. Maybe he was my last link to my best friend, something I wasn't ready to let go of.

Jake dropped me off back at Tom's place and I sat reading for the rest of the day. The talk with Jake had helped, but I still couldn't let go of that need to know. The thought that Callie had been trying to reach out for help haunted me.

Most of the journal entries were the same thing.

Callie talked a lot about her depression. In a way, I thought writing the journal was an outlet for her. As I continued to read it became very clear that she felt she couldn't talk to anyone about what she was feeling. The one person she had told, other than me, had used it against her.

Callie had left the supermarket two years after getting the job there. Fortunately, the matter with the man who had been harassing her had sorted itself out when someone else had gone to the store manager complaining of sexual harassment. It was something which had become a very big deal in the past fifteen years.

I had moved to Dunedin for four years to study for a health sciences degree. The university was one of only two in the country that offered the degree, the other being in Auckland, and that city just hadn't appealed. Dunedin was not quite as large as Auckland, and much colder than I was used to, since it snowed in winter, but I grew to like it there, even if I would never love it the same way I loved the city I had grown up in. I moved in with two others, who were also students, and both familiar with the city, which helped immensely.

Separated by living at different ends of the country, Callie and I missed each other terribly, but I had always thought she understood that I had few options. I wondered if she had resented the fact that I had chosen a city so far away from her, but there had only been resignation in her journal entries.

Still, we kept in touch, first by letter, then by email. Occasionally we'd phone, but since Callie didn't have much money, she tried to keep the phone calls to a minimum to avoid huge phone bills.

I was initially worried when she told me she was moving to Auckland. I'd passed through the city on my way north for a conference, but I hadn't actually visited the city since I was very small.

The job she had moved to Auckland for paid minimum wage but she had seemed happy enough with it. Little did I know that she was struggling to keep her head above water. She was flatting with another girl and two guys, who were students at Auckland University. The three of them spent more time partying than they did studying and were always trying to get Callie to go clubbing with them. It had never been her scene so she had always told them no.

It was supposed to have been equal share in the flat, but Callie ended up paying most of the bills. Her flatmates would eat her food and then complain they never had money to buy groceries themselves. Yet, the only place she ever complained about it was in her journal.

Things finally came to a head about six months after she moved in when she learned that the flatmate who was supposed to be paying the rent hadn't paid anything for weeks. The landlord had kicked them all out, refusing to give Callie a reference. She had basically been lumped in with the others and judged equally to blame for the loud music and the mess, no matter how much she had tried to get them to stop.

Desperate to find a better situation, she had asked around at the office and a co-worker had offered a room. Callie had initially been happy to have been able to get a room so quickly and she had moved in. A month or so after she had related all this in the journal, I read another entry.

Ugh, I thought living with the dastardly trio was bad enough, Amber is proving to be the flatmate from hell. I have absolutely no privacy. She just barges into my room to 'borrow' my clothes, without asking, then either ruins them or dumps them back in my room stinking of cigarette smoke.

Don't get me started on the food. She claims we're supposed to be sharing the food but she eats way more than me, then refuses to pay for what I feel is equal to her share. She hates it when I buy food for myself, saying it's rude that I don't share it with her, but how else am I going to be able to have something for myself?

She keeps telling me I shouldn't eat so much and that I'm fat and ugly. Yet Mrs B in the office keeps saying I'm too skinny!

But this ... this was the final straw. Amber barged into my room once again and she had clearly been rifling through my drawers as she showed me the tablets the doctor gave me.

"What's this?" she asked.

I frowned at her. "Medication."

"For what? Are you sick? I'm not good around sick people."

"It's just Prozac," I said.

"What's Prozac?" she said, frowning.

I didn't want to tell her that it was an anti-depressant. It really was none of her business. I didn't even want to be on the stuff in the first place, but the doctor had insisted. Anyway, she kept pushing, so I told her the truth.

The next day I got called in to the boss' office. He got

straight to the point. Amber must have told him I had 'issues'. I mean, he never said so, but I overheard her talking to someone, saying I nuts, or bipolar or something. He didn't come straight out and say it. I guess they can't anyway, for fear they would be accused of discrimination, so he made it sound like it wasn't working out. They were letting me go. He tried to make it sound like it wasn't about my illness, but it had to be the real reason.

So, guess I'm unemployed again. And homeless. I can't stay with Amber, not after what she did to me.

She tried to pretend that she was sorry for me and wanted to help me find another job. But I just can't trust her now.

Reading that made me so angry. Maybe they weren't blatant about it, but to me it read like discrimination. Especially if Amber had told them about the medication. There was a possibility Callie had been wrong but I had a feeling her instincts had been right. Especially when she talked about how Amber treated her. It was like Jake had said earlier. People either didn't understand it or pretended it didn't exist. Or when they did, they saw it as something to be afraid of.

Would they have seen things differently if Callie had been honest with them from the start? It was hard to say. Honesty wasn't always the best policy, but lying, even to protect herself, clearly didn't do Callie any favours either. It wasn't fair. It looked like Callie wasn't going to be able to win no matter what she did.

I'd read enough about depression to know there was still a lot of misinformation out there. I was beginning to understand more about why Callie chose not to tell anyone the extent of her illness. What she had told me was barely the tip of the iceberg.

People treated her differently when they found out she was sick. Did she think I would do that to her?

Had she died because she could no longer live with that fear?

CHAPTER TWENTY

Tom came home late that evening. He didn't talk about work, although I could tell there was something bothering him. He was quiet as he sat down in the living room with a can of beer.

"Everything okay?" I asked.

He shrugged, clearly not ready to tell me what was wrong. He spotted the journal I'd been reading on the coffee table and frowned at me.

"Why are you still reading the journals?" he asked, sounding more curious than scolding.

"Because I need to know. I need to reassure myself that it wasn't my fault."

He looked confused. "How could it be your fault, Janet? You didn't give her the pills. From what you've told me, you were nothing but supportive. I wish you wouldn't," he said, sighing. "I'm worried about you. I mean, your boss wouldn't have told you to take time off if it wasn't affecting your work."

"I know, Tommy. I know you're worried."

He must have caught the note in my voice as he looked at me. I nodded.

"I took a walk and ran into Jake. He told me you and he and been talking about things." He started to open his mouth to say something and I put a hand up to stop him. "I'm not mad, Tommy. I get that you've been worried about me. Anyway, it helped to talk to someone who was kind of impartial."

"I'm sorry," he said. "I thought ..." He sighed again, sipping from his can. "I don't know what I thought."

"It's really okay," I told him. "You have nothing to apologise for. I mean, at first I wasn't sure about talking to him, but he seemed like a nice guy."

"He is," Tom said. "He used to work as a counsellor at the hospital but now writes a column for one of the local rags and works freelance. He's had a lot of experience at this. I guess ... I guess I just needed someone who, as you said, was impartial."

I nibbled on my finger. It was a habit I'd picked up in childhood when I was nervous or worried. My mother had often told me off for biting my nails and I'd started nibbling on the tips of my finger instead.

"I just need you to understand that this is something I have to do," I said, indicating the journal on the table. "As painful as it is, reading what she was going through, I still need this. It's like reading a book that you know the ending to, but you still want to see how it led to that conclusion."

"Are you thinking that something made her do this?" he asked.

I thought about it for a second, then nodded.

"I think so. I mean, Callie wrote about a lot of painful stuff. She made it through all of that, so I want to know what happened to make her feel that she had no other choice."

He looked down and took my hand, squeezing it gently.

"Okay," he said. "I get where you're coming from. But promise me you will talk to me or someone like Jake if it all starts to get too much. Okay?"

"I promise," I said, turning my hand over to squeeze him back.

He eventually told me he'd had an argument with Callie's old manager after he'd found some irregularities in the accounts. It was fairly clear he didn't like the man, but felt there was little he could really do about it. Phil had claimed the irregularities had just been a mistake and become belligerent when Tom told him he was going to go to their boss about it. The man's attitude had caused Tom, who was not usually given to violence, to want to smack him.

Talking about it seemed to help him relax and let go of the tension he'd obviously been feeling since he'd walked in the door. He admitted he had also been a little worried I might be hurt or angry that he had felt the need to talk about me with Jake and was relieved when I wasn't.

He didn't ask me about the journals over the next day or so and the subject was left to rest. For him, anyway. I continued to read, growing ever more concerned about the things I was reading.

Callie had managed to get another job three months after she was fired from the other job and she had learned her lesson. She kept things very much to herself, refusing to volunteer any kind of personal information. Her medication was well-hidden and she had learned not to trust anyone, not even her new flatmates.

She had found the job through an agency, which had asked her why she was 'let go'. She noted in her journal that she hadn't told them her suspicions and the subject was never brought up by her new boss. I didn't think it was legal for the company to divulge such information anyway, even if they had let her go because of her health problems.

Callie's entries became shorter and there were greater gaps between. In the earlier journals, she had made entries nearly every day, but in the few I had read, sometimes it was every second day; other times it was once a week.

I had to wonder if the medication she was taking was having a detrimental effect on her mind, or whether it was the sickness taking hold. The entries seemed disjointed. Callie had always prided herself on using proper grammar. Maybe it wasn't perfect, but she had always been better at it than I was. Yet I found myself barely able to read. It was almost as if she was writing one thought and moving on to the next in the middle of writing it down. Her thoughts seemed scattered and her writing, while never exactly neat, which I thought was the product of someone whose brain worked faster than they could write, became downright messy and much harder to read. Certainly not what anyone could call legible.

Sometimes she would just write a short sentence. *I hate my life*. Or: *I hate my job*. No details. Nothing to tell me what was going on in her mind. This went on for some years, until she got the job at the last company she worked for.

When I thought about those years, I couldn't recall Callie ever talking to me about it.

The first I knew she was sick was when she came down to visit her parents. I had been at my job about a year or so and while I was still a little unsure of myself in terms of working with the clients, I liked my boss. Alex had made it so easy for me to just go to him when I needed guidance.

Callie had decided to stay with her parents for about a week or so and of course we spent an entire weekend catching up. I had offered for her to stay at my place overnight. I hadn't bought my little house then, as I was still saving for a deposit, but my flatmates had gone away for the weekend. I hadn't known then that they had begun dating a few weeks earlier. They're married now, with three children, and are both very happy together.

Since I was on my own that weekend, it was no bother at all to have Callie stay over. We stayed up until late that Saturday night just talking. I had noticed that Callie seemed a little listless but she hadn't said anything and I had been reluctant to bring it up. Still, it was bothering me.

"Cal?"

"Mm?" she said, lifting her head to look at me.

"Is everything okay?"

She bit her lip, a sure sign she was trying to stop herself from saying too much, then shrugged.

"Fine. Why?"

I sighed. "C'mon Cal, we've known each other way

too long. I know when something's not right."

"It's fine, really," she said stubbornly.

I felt she was trying to get me to drop it, rather than denying it, but I couldn't drop it. I was worried about her.

"Callie, talk to me. Please," I said quietly. "I've been thinking for a while something's going on and I can't help you if you don't tell me."

"Jannie, please just drop it," she said, using the nickname she'd come up with for me when we were kids. Just as I always called her Cal.

"I can't." I couldn't help thinking of all the times she had acted evasive on the phone, sounded a little down, or refusing to talk about various things that were going on in her life.

I didn't want to drop the subject.

"Cal, what happened with that job?"

"Which job?"

"The data entry one."

She shrugged. Again. I could see how some people would find that annoying. It was an answer but it wasn't an answer. It wasn't an 'I don't know' kind of shrug. It was a 'whatever' shrug. Yet I didn't think it was because Callie didn't care.

"Callie, what happened?"

"Nothing. It just didn't work out, that's all."

"Cal …"

"Janet, just leave it alone!" she said, practically exploding. She got up from the couch and walked out, clearly refusing to discuss the matter further.

We'd had arguments before, but Callie had never blown up at me like that. It told me something was really wrong.

I knew I had to let the matter drop until she was ready to talk about it. The question was, would she ever be ready to talk about it?

I went to bed that night feeling upset and more than a little worried about Callie, who was pretending to sleep beside me. She had offered to sleep on the couch, but I knew how uncomfortable it was and it was no big deal. We'd had plenty of sleepovers when we were kids. I tossed and turned for a while, but I was too restless to sleep.

After what seemed like an hour or so, I heard her quiet voice in the darkness.

"Janet, I'm sorry. It's just … I can't talk about it."

"Why not? Cal, you're my best friend. If something's wrong, tell me. I know we can fix it."

"This isn't something you can fix," she said with a sigh.

"You're not … you're not, you know, sick, or anything," I said. "Are you?"

"Um, I guess it depends on your definition. I guess you could say I'm sick, but some people think it's not."

"Not what? Not an illness?"

Okay, I thought. So it's not cancer or anything like that. She would have said so.

She took a deep breath and told me what was wrong. She talked for what seemed like an hour. I listened, wanting to ask questions, but knowing how difficult it was for her to even admit to having had problems. The last thing she needed was to be bombarded with more questions about what she was going through.

I hugged her.

"Thank you for telling me. I'm glad you did."

"You don't think I'm stupid for, you know, for this?"

"No, I don't," I told her firmly. "And anyone who does think so is an idiot. This is not something you can just get over and I hate anyone who says that."

She started to cry then and all I could do was put my arms around my friend and hold her.

"I'm sorry," she said, between sobs. "I don't want to be a b-burden."

"You are not a burden. You're my best friend and I love you and I don't want to hear you say that. Like I said, I'm glad you told me what was going on. I'm the one who should be sorry for not saying something sooner."

"Love you too, Janet," she said softly, her sobs subsiding.

I wanted to say something to try to lighten the moment, but there was just nothing I could say except that I would always be there to be a friend when she needed one.

Callie had written about that night in her journal and it felt to me like she was relieved. Not only for telling me, but because I hadn't reacted at all as she had imagined. She admitted thinking that I would see her differently once I knew, but I could never do that. I was upset, but not angry at her for feeling that way.

I wished I could say that her confession made things easier between us, but it didn't. Callie never brought up the subject again and while I continued to ask her how things were, she never seemed to want to discuss her illness. It felt like she went back to hiding behind those walls she had always kept up to protect herself and not even I could get through.

I'd tried to talk to her parents about it, but they both had seemed uncomfortable. I was given the strong impression that they were one of the main reasons Callie had chosen to hide her illness.

I sighed as I put down the journal I was reading and got up to make myself a coffee. I stretched, getting rid of the kinks in my back. I'd become so absorbed in reading I hadn't realised how much time had passed, but as I looked at the clock, I saw it was almost three.

Tom had called around noon asking if I wanted to meet him at his office. While I wasn't overly eager to see the place Callie had worked and meet the kind of people she had worked with, a part of me was curious to know what kind of people could be so caught up in their own lives that they hadn't seen that something was seriously wrong with my friend.

Tom had told me they were having a social evening, where they could invite friends. They would all be meeting at the office first before going on to the café and bar.

At around quarter to five I parked my car in the car park and got out, entering the building and approached the reception desk. The woman at the desk was about ten years younger than me, with long blonde hair tied up in a loose ponytail and freckles dotted in random spots on her face.

"Can I help you?" she asked, friendly, but not too friendly. The tone was polite but not inviting confidences. I detected an accent which I figured to be South African.

"Hi," I said. "I'm Janet. A friend of Tom McFadden."

Her eyes widened as she stared at me, then shook herself. To my surprise, she came around the end of the desk and gave me a huge hug.

"I'm so sorry about Callie," she said. "I didn't find out about it until a couple of days after the funeral. I was on holiday, in Melbourne, actually." Then she sent me a sheepish look. "Gosh, you must think I'm a lunatic or something," she added with an embarrassed laugh. "Uh, I'm Melissa. Callie talked about you a lot."

She quickly explained that she and Callie had talked often, which seemed a little unusual, until she confided that she had been having troubles with a boyfriend and Callie had provided a sympathetic ear. I couldn't help thinking that Melissa was another one of my friend's 'strays'.

She led me through the building and up the stairs to meet Tom, chattering all the way. She seemed like a nice person and I could see why Callie had taken her under her wing, so to speak. As we walked, I could see the puzzled stares from some of the people in the office.

Tom looked up from his desk and smiled at me.

"Hey, you made it," he said. "We're just finishing up."

Melissa smiled as Tom asked her if she was going to join us later. She nodded, patted my shoulder and turned to go back to the reception desk.

Another man approached Tom's desk and looked me up and down. He sneered at me.

"Who's this?" he asked rudely.

"This is Janet. Callie's friend," Tom said pointedly,

glaring at the man. "This is Phil. He was Callie's boss."

I looked him up and down the same way he had looked at me. Like he'd been found wanting. He would have been good-looking if it wasn't for the arrogant smirk or the way he glared back at me like he smelled something bad. Poor Callie, I thought. If this is what she had to work with I didn't blame her for being upset.

He snorted and turned away, going back to whatever hole he had crawled out from.

"So, that's Phil," I said. "I'm not surprised Callie disliked him. He acted like he had a huge stick up his butt when I talked to him on the phone. I can see he still acts like that."

Tom grinned and nodded. I heard footsteps behind me and turned to look at a tall, red-haired woman. She was aged in her forties, her hair just beginning to show signs of greying, although that was never a good indication of age. I frowned, thinking she looked familiar, then remembered she had come to the funeral. She had been not only Callie and Phil's boss, but she was manager of the whole division.

"Hello Janet," she said with a smile. "Tom said you'd come to stay with him a few days."

I nodded. "Hi Kim," I said, relieved that I'd remembered her name. While there hadn't been that many people at the service, it was still difficult figuring out who was whom.

Kim put some documents down on Tom's desk.

"Why don't you come down to my office while Tom finishes up," she said, her tone friendly but not without meaning. Tom shrugged and smiled as he picked up the documents and began to read them.

I followed Kim to her office. Unlike the rest of the team, which sat in little cubicles, Kim had a fairly large office with a comfortable couch. She sat down, relaxing against the arm of the couch, gesturing for me to sit beside her.

"So how are you doing, really?" she asked.

"I'm okay. Taking it one day at a time."

"Tom mentioned you've been spending a lot of time reading Callie's journals."

"He told you?" I asked, surprised.

She grinned at me. "Some of the team say I act like their mother sometimes, even though I'm not the oldest one here." She sighed softly. "I'm sorry, I don't want to sound like I'm poking my nose in where it's not wanted, although it really does sound like that, doesn't it?"

"It's okay," I said. "You're concerned."

"What happened to Callie was a shock to all of us. I thought a lot of her. She was extremely good at her job, even though I know it wasn't what she wanted to do with her life. The thing about Callie was she always gave one hundred and ten percent, even if she hated what she was doing."

I nodded. That sounded like her.

"She kept a lot of things to herself, and I have to admit I was worried. She was getting upset over little things and we all thought there was something going on but we could never get her to talk about it."

"But you don't know what it was?" I asked. "The thing is, I've been trying to figure that out myself. I'm just trying to understand what made her do what she did."

Kim nodded. "I understand. I keep thinking the same things myself. There are times when I wonder if I should have pushed more for her to get help."

I didn't know if that would have changed anything. Somehow, I didn't think so. Later that night, as I was reading the journal in bed, I found another entry in the journal that told me exactly why she didn't want to talk about it. She had been at her job for two years and had written a long entry about it, sounding so down.

I really hate my job. I feel like I'm being used and abused and I don't think I'm getting paid enough for what I do. It just feels like I'm not going to get anywhere in this job, like my manager doesn't want to promote me. I've been here two years. I've been trying to apply for other jobs but I don't even get replies.

She did talk about Kim and I could tell that she wanted to talk to her about what was going on. She at least understood that Kim was really only trying to help her and wasn't about to penalise her for not liking her job. If anything, from the little talk I'd had with Kim in her office, I thought the manager had hoped by being supportive that Callie would confide in her. She clearly cared about her staff and far from not appreciating what Callie did, she admired my friend for her work ethic.

I wondered if Callie had perhaps taken it the wrong way as she seemed to get even more upset after Kim had called her into the office and talked to her once again about getting some help, even offering to put her in touch with a counsellor.

Why me? Why does this stuff always happen to me? It's

so unfair! Am I a jinx or something? Is that why my parents have always had so many problems?

While it appeared she hadn't taken Kim up on her offer, she had tried to get help another way, by contacting someone or joining a forum.

I tried talking to someone but it seemed like they weren't willing to meet me halfway. I don't even know why I bothered even trying. It's too hard. I can't deal with this anymore.

I even tried asking for help online but nobody replied to my post. Why? Am I really such a loser that people don't want to know, or don't even care? Why do other people get replies but not me?

I know I should talk to Janet, but even though she says I'm not a burden, I kind of think I am. I mean, she's got a great job, and good friends. Why would she want to waste her time with me? All I ever do is bring her down. I don't want her to think that I only call her when I want something.

It seems like whenever we talk, all I ever do is complain to her about how much my life sucks.

That was not true at all, I thought as I read what she had written. Callie had barely said a word to me about how bad things were, or how she was feeling.

I have to stick it out, Callie wrote, and I knew it was that stubborn pride of hers talking again. Callie's mother used to say that both Callie and her father had a stubborn streak a mile wide and I could definitely see that at play.

Part of me wanted to cry out as I sat up in bed, my back propped against the pillows, wanting to ask what was so different about the last time that her pride and her stubbornness had failed her. I couldn't. I didn't want to disturb Tom or Miranda, sleeping in the next room.

Callie continued on, writing about how helpless she felt to do anything about her life. It hurt that she didn't want to talk to me. I knew she didn't want to be a burden, but nonetheless it still hurt that she had felt that way.

Her anger and her pain was there for me to see and it was overwhelming. I started to cry, without even being aware that it was happening until I felt strong arms around me, holding me gently but firmly.

Tom spoke what seemed like soothing words in my ear but I was too deep into my own pain to understand him.

It felt like once I had started crying I couldn't stop. This wasn't a normal cry, but deep wracking sobs that I felt like an ache in my bones. I cried until my face hurt and my eyes burned.

Tom just held me the entire time, his hands rubbing up and down my back. He didn't seem to care that I'd soaked his t-shirt with my tears, or that my face was red and my eyes were swelling. He just continued to stroke my back, his big hands applying gentle pressure.

"Let it out, Janet," he said softly. "Let it out."

CHAPTER TWENTY-ONE

I had no idea how long it had been since he'd come in, but even when my sobs finally subsided he made no mention of it. I pulled away, gazing up at him, not sure what to say or how to act. He was so close, all I could do was stare at his full lips wondering what it would be like to kiss him.

It sounded stupid, considering I'd just been crying over my best friend, but in that moment it was all I could think about. His thumb was brushing my cheek, gently wiping the trail of tears and I felt a tiny frisson up and down my spine.

He stopped stroking, looking down at me, his eyes widening slightly. I wondered if he was feeling the same way I was. His eyes began to do an odd little dance and I again felt a tiny quiver. I had never looked directly into his eyes before, and the light was a little dim, but they were the deepest azure blue I had ever seen. Callie had had blue eyes but hers had been a much lighter shade. So light in fact that in direct sunlight they seemed almost clear.

His lips pressing against mine was not unwelcome,

but I jerked back a little in surprise. Maybe I had been thinking about it, but I hadn't expected him to actually kiss me.

The kiss was gentle. He didn't push, didn't force the kiss on me and was clearly prepared to pull back if it wasn't what I wanted. After my initial hesitation, I responded, opening my mouth in invitation. He seemed encouraged by the response, deepening the embrace by holding me in his arms.

To my surprise, he suddenly pulled back, looking down.

"I'm sorry," he said.

I frowned at him. "For what?"

"I shouldn't have done that."

"Kiss me?" I asked.

He nodded. "You're grieving, Janet."

"It's not wrong," I replied. "I wanted it too." I inhaled deeply, getting a slight whiff of the soap he had used in the shower. He smelled fresh and clean and in many ways I felt like I wanted to wrap my arms around him, lay my head on his chest and just breathe him in.

"Janet, I ..."

"Tommy, I know we hardly know each other, except for talking on the phone. I mean, I probably shouldn't have even come here, but I just ... I needed to be around someone who knew Callie the way I did. I mean, her flatmate, I know they were friends, but sometimes I just felt like she never knew her." I was babbling but I felt like he was pulling away. "I guess I knew that I could trust you." I paused and looked at him. "There's something between us. I know you feel it too.”

He bit his lip. “You’re right. I do feel … something. But …”

“It’s not wrong,” I repeated. “If anything, what happened to Callie should be a reason for us to embrace whatever it is. Give it a chance to grow into something more, rather than dismiss it. Tommy, if Callie’s death has taught me anything, it’s that life is short, too short to worry about what ifs.”

I looked up at him, my eyes pleading with him. I didn’t know if it would lead somewhere. All I knew was that I couldn’t just dismiss these feelings. I knew instinctively that this was something Callie would want for me.

“I want to, Janet,” he confessed. “I’m just not sure …”

“Why did you ask me up here?” I pointed out.

He had no answer to that, just as I knew he wouldn’t. I thought he must have rationalised things in his head, telling himself that he was just trying to help, when it was really more than that. He felt something, just like I did, but he wasn’t ready to admit his feelings even to himself.

I knew that I would have to make the first move. I had known it all along.

“Tommy …”

He rose from the bed.

“I should make some tea,” he said.

“Don’t avoid the subject,” I replied.

“I’m not. I just … I think we need to talk more about this. I don’t know about you, but I’d rather talk over a cup of tea.”

I tried a wan smile. "All right, but you're not getting off the hook that easy mister."

He smiled back at me. "You sound so much like Callie when you do that."

While he went to make the tea, I went to the bathroom, washing my face with a damp facecloth. I glanced at my reflection in the mirror. My eyes were red from crying, the skin puffy underneath. I looked a mess.

Sighing, I dried my face and opened the bathroom door to find Tom on his way back out bearing a tray with two mugs of steaming tea. He smiled tentatively at me. I shrugged.

"I'm a mess," I said.

"No you're not," he replied, shaking his head.

I followed him into the bedroom and sat on the bed as he set the tray down on the bedside table. I crossed my legs, leaning back against the pillows, waiting for him to sit beside me. Instead he grabbed the stool which normally sat in the corner.

"Is that the first time you've really grieved?" he asked.

"I cried at the funeral," I said.

"Yeah, but that's normal. Have you really actually grieved for Callie?"

I considered his meaning for a few moments. He was right. Maybe I had broken down at the funeral, but in many ways I hadn't let myself grieve for Callie. I had gone back to work and got on with things, trying not to think about what I had lost. Crying at a funeral, especially when it had been for someone I was so close to, wasn't really grieving. In many ways, it was just a reaction to the stress of everything.

Grief took time. Even I knew that in my limited psychology skills. I had spent so much time trying to understand why I had lost Callie, I had never really let myself feel the loss.

"I guess I haven't," I said, looking up at him, noticing the concern in his expression.

He handed me the hot tea, picking up his own mug.

"Janet, I know I wasn't as close to Callie as you were, and I'm no psychologist, but I find myself wondering why."

"Why what?"

"Why you've spent so much time running away from your feelings," he said quietly. "I mean, I know it was my suggestion for you to come up here and stay, but ..."

"Why did you?" I asked, conscious of the fact that I'd asked him that question not five minutes earlier.

"Part of me wanted to help." He shrugged and sighed. "Another part of me felt ... I don't know. It sounds weird in my head, but I guess I felt a connection to you."

"That doesn't sound weird," I told him. I'd felt that same connection.

"I don't know what this is, Janet. You're right. There is something between us. But I don't want to confuse the issue."

"I'm not confused," I replied.

He sipped his tea absently, looking as if he was trying to find the right words.

"Janet, I haven't had that many relationships. I know it sounds odd, coming from me."

"It's not," I answered, remembering my talk with Jake. "I've always known you were kind of reticent." I reached out and put a hand on his knee. "I haven't had that many relationships either, FYI."

"Why not? You're a beautiful woman. You're smart, gregarious ..."

I smiled at the compliment. "I guess I just never found the right person who understood me."

"Well, you are kind of weird," he replied with a mischievous grin, poking my knee with his finger.

"Hey!" I said with mock indignation, pretending to scowl at him.

He raised his hand in surrender.

"Kidding!"

I narrowed my eyes at him. "You, mister McFadden, are trouble."

He cocked an eyebrow. "Who? Me?"

"Yes, you."

He tried for an innocent look.

"Must be thinking of someone else."

"Yeah right!" I muttered, sipping my tea. He'd made it perfectly. Just the right strength with the perfect balance of sweetness.

He laughed. I again thought how much I liked his laugh. Deep and throaty, his whole face engaged, from the wide grin showing even, white teeth, to his eyes crinkling in the corners.

We sat and talked for a little while, about anything but Callie. I told him about some funnier incidents that had happened at work, which he seemed to enjoy.

The tea was long gone and my eyes were drooping when we finally said goodnight. Tom moved to pick up the tray, then looked at me. He seemed to be considering something. Not wanting to break the mood, I said nothing. Tom leaned over and kissed me briefly on the lips.

"Goodnight Janet," he said.

He left the room, closing the door quietly, and I settled down to sleep. Despite how tired I was, I lay awake for a little while, going over the things Tom had said in my mind. Had I really been running away from my feelings? What was I afraid of?

I didn't really have an answer. Maybe he was partially right. Maybe I had been avoiding my feelings about Callie's death, but the thought that it could have been my fault, even just a little, was too painful to bear. It was irrational, I knew that deep down. As Jake had told me, it was never that simple.

When I went out the next morning, Tom had clearly already been up for a while. Since it was Saturday, he didn't have to go to work, so I wondered where he was. I went to grab some cereal for breakfast when I heard the front door slam.

Miranda came in, looking sweaty and flushed.

"Hey," she said, smiling brightly.

She went to the fridge and grabbed the bottle of juice, picking up a glass from the shelf and pouring some of the juice.

"Been out for a run?" I asked as I poured muesli into a bowl.

"Yeah. It's getting cold out there," she said.

I nodded, grabbing the plastic container of milk from the fridge and pouring some on my cereal. Miranda frowned at me.

"How can you drink that stuff?" she asked.

I blinked at her, wondering what she meant. She shrugged.

"I never liked milk. My mum used to tell me I got really sick when I was little."

I nodded. It sounded like she was lactose intolerant. I wasn't sure how many people were, but it was a fairly common complaint.

"Well, I grew up on a dairy farm until I was seven, so ..." I shrugged. I'd never really thought anything of it. Despite learning a little bit about nutrition and different food allergies when I'd been studying for my degree.

She looked thoughtful as she leaned back against the bench, glass of juice in one hand.

"What was it like? Growing up on a dairy farm?"

"The same as a normal childhood, I guess. I mean, I was just a kid, so I didn't have too many chores. I visit my dad now and again and help out on the farm." I smiled at her. "My dad's pretty cool. So is my grandad. He's in his nineties now, but I still remember going to stay in the summer and sitting out on the porch listening to him singing."

She seemed a little envious and I knew why. I supposed my childhood must have seemed idyllic by comparison to hers. At least her mother had protected her by getting them out of a bad situation.

I'd heard of so many children in similar situations going off the rails, but she seemed like a good kid.

Miranda finished her juice and put the glass in the sink. She had told me that Tom was a bit of a neat freak who didn't like to see dirty dishes out on the bench, and would wash them as soon as he saw them, but she was slowly trying to break him out of the habit.

"I heard you and Tom talking last night," she said, watching as I ate my cereal.

"Oh yeah?"

"Yeah. It's not your fault, you know? About Callie, I mean."

"I don't know," I said with a sigh.

"It wasn't," she insisted. "Callie was sick. She would be hurt if she thought she was causing you this much pain. I mean, when my Mum was sick, she tried to hide the fact that she was in pain from me, but I always knew. Just like I knew why. She was trying to protect me."

I wanted to tell her she was wrong, but she had been through her own pain. First with her father's abuse and her mother's illness, Callie, then her mother's death, in such a short time. This fifteen-year-old girl knew more about pain than I possibly could.

"Callie told me a lot of stuff. She understood what I was going through with my Mum. I mean, okay, not everything, but it's like she knew what Mum went through."

I frowned at her, wondering what she meant by that. Had Callie been through some kind of abuse?

"What exactly did Callie say?" I asked, hoping to get some more information from Miranda.

"Just that she had this illness that made her sad sometimes, and she knew what it was like to struggle with something she had no control over. She and my Mum used to talk about my Dad and what he did."

The way she talked implied there was a lot more to it than she was saying. I wondered, was she trying to protect Callie's memory by not saying anything? As much as I wanted the answers, I had a feeling that pushing for the answers wasn't the right thing to do.

"Do you ever talk to your father?" I asked.

Miranda shook her head. "I don't even see him. He's too busy getting drunk, or doing drugs."

I nodded. Tom had told me that that had been part of the reason Miranda had been able to live independently, albeit with adult supervision.

"Tom went out to get some groceries and stuff," she said. "He didn't want to wake you up. Especially after last night." She bit her lip, looking like she was considering something. "You know, I kind of told him he should ask you out. I know he likes you, Janet."

"I like him too."

"It's like you said last night," she continued, making it clear she had heard almost every word. "Life's too short to think about what if. I mean, maybe it'll turn out to be nothing, but maybe it won't. I just ... with my Mum and everything, I know how short life is. Sometimes you just have to take a chance. You never know what might happen."

She was right about that. If I had learned anything from the past few weeks, it was that.

Miranda smiled at me and told me she was going to take a shower and get ready for work. She usually worked a double shift on weekends at the restaurant. It wasn't a job she enjoyed, but she had figured that at least it was a job and the small amount she earned would go toward her education. She hadn't decided what she was going to do with her life, but getting a university degree was top on her list of priorities. It was one of the things she had promised her mother.

As she left the kitchen, I heard a footstep behind me and turned. Tom had clearly been there a while.

"Sorry," he said. "I didn't want to wake you up."

"It's okay," I replied.

"Good. So, uh, I've been thinking. Would you like to maybe go out with me?"

"On a date?"

He tried for a disarming smile. "Is that what they call it?"

"Okay, can the sarcasm," I replied.

"So, will you? We could go to the movies, or whatever."

"Movies sounds good," I answered.

He smiled, looking almost relieved. "Good. Great."

CHAPTER TWENTY-TWO

We decided on a movie which wasn't a blockbuster but one which would at least act as a little bit of a distraction from our own worries. I'd told Tom that I wasn't much into what they called 'chick flicks'. I supposed they had their place, and they were certainly popular with some people, but to me they tended to be trite and over-emotional.

I liked movies that made me think. That said something about the human condition. Or movies that were semi-biographical. The movie we'd decided to see was based on real-life events in the Middle East about twenty years ago. Obviously while some of them had really happened, the writer had taken poetic licence with a few things.

I'd seen the trailer for it and thought it looked interesting and when Tom had suggested going out to the movies I'd suggested that one, hoping I'd be able to become so absorbed in what was happening on screen I wouldn't worry about what ifs with Tom.

It wasn't enough of a distraction. I sat in that darkened theatre wondering what was going to happen next between Tom and I. We'd taken the first step toward seeing where this could go. Was I ready to take that step?

Maybe it was contradictory to what I'd said to him the night before, but I'd been down that road before and all of my other relationships hadn't ended well. In many ways, because of all that I'd already shared with Tom, I really didn't want to make the same mistake with him that I'd made with all the others I'd gone out with.

I began thinking about the men I'd dated in the past. There had been a guy I'd met at university who had been taking drugs, and another fellow student at Otago University who I had gone out with for about two years. Dion had been a decent enough guy although he had been more interested in his studies than in having a girlfriend. If I was honest with myself, I had been more than a little relieved when he'd broken up with me.

Since then I'd gone out with maybe three more guys, two of whom hadn't really been relationship material. While one of them had been nice, I hadn't felt any kind of spark with him. Tom was the first man I'd ever felt such an attraction to.

I knew what my decision was going to be. I'd be taking a chance but the last thing I wanted was to walk away without ever having at least given it a shot.

I tried to concentrate on the movie, but having him so close beside me just proved to be too much of a different kind of distraction.

He reached out and squeezed my hand and I realised he was feeling the same way. I looked at him and offered a smile, hoping he saw it in the dim light from the screen. His answering squeeze told me he did.

Thankfully the movie wasn't all that long and we left the theatre as the credits rolled. Tom grinned at me.

"So, do they have any sort of nightlife in Napier?" he asked.

"Bars, cafes. Why?"

"Ever been clubbing?"

I shook my head. "Not really. I mean, I did go out a few times when I was at Otago, but I've never really been a nightclub kind of person."

I doubted the clubs in Dunedin were anything like he was talking about.

"Never?" he asked, raising an eyebrow.

"What are you thinking?" I asked.

"I thought you might like to check out one of the clubs here. There are a couple that don't play bad music. That's if you're up to the challenge."

I fluttered my eyelashes at him.

"Mr McFadden, are you daring me?" I asked.

He leaned close to me so his lips were brushing my cheek as he spoke in my ear.

"What would you say if I was?"

I pulled away slightly and grinned back at him.

"I never back down from a challenge," I replied.

"Is that so? So, Ms Kingi, you ready?"

"Lead on MacDuff," I said with a laugh.

Tom drove in to the central city. As he followed along the highway, I could see the Sky Tower in the distance. It stood out against the night sky even with the surrounding buildings lit brightly. The tower was supposedly the tallest man-made structure in the country.

I didn't dare ask where we were going as I assumed he knew the way. He parked the car down a side street and looked at me as he turned off the ignition.

"Sorry. We have to walk a little way. It's hard to get parking so close to the club."

"That's okay," I said. I got out of the car and followed him down the street to what appeared to be the main street. We still had to walk a few metres until I heard the sounds of music and people chattering. Tom glanced at me, then took my hand as we joined the line of people waiting to get in.

It wasn't like this in Napier, I thought. Bars there did tend to get crowded, but apart from a man at the door to check people's ages, there was no lining up.

"Why do they line up?" I asked Tom.

"So they don't over-crowd the club," he explained. "It's all to do with fire safety regulations and I forget what else, but yeah, it's for public safety."

"Oh." I smiled sheepishly. "Is it that obvious I don't do this much?"

He smiled back at me. "Just a tad." He had a teasing look on his face and didn't appear to be bothered by it.

I could hear the club playing music from the eighties. It was music that was comforting, in a way, as it was familiar. Callie and I had both preferred pop as opposed to rock'n'roll although she had liked hip hop style as well, whereas I'd never been able to stand listening to it for very long.

She had once told me I was a bit of a 'fuddy-duddy'

for not getting in to the more modern music. Then she'd laughed, assuring me that she'd only been teasing.

We were let inside the club and Tom found us a table, offering to get us both a drink. I opted for a light beer, wanting something with a bit less alcohol. Tom made a face.

"Light beer? That's a sacrilege," he teased.

I screwed my nose up at him. "You'll live," I said.

He laughed, going off to get the drinks. I sat at the table, listening to the music and the chatter around me without really registering what people were saying.

Callie had once told me her flatmate, before she'd moved in with Susan, had dragged her to a nightclub for New Year's, then pretty much abandoned her by going off with a group of people Callie hadn't known. She had tried to have fun anyway by joining in on some of the dancing, but the music hadn't been to her taste and there had been too many people. She'd stumbled and nearly fell over when someone had pushed someone else in the crowd and she'd left well before midnight, disgusted with her flatmate for leaving her alone.

"Your light beer, madame," Tom said, putting on a fake French accent.

I rolled my eyes at him. "That's terrible," I said.

"Ahh sue me," he said, sipping his own beer. "I was too lazy to take French at school."

He sat on the stool beside me.

"What were you thinking about just now?" he asked. "You had a very serious look on your face."

"Oh, just something Callie told me once. Her

flatmate took her to a club once but then took off with some friends."

"A few of the guys at the office asked her to go out with them but she never did." He sighed softly. "A couple of them, like Becca and Julie, tried to get her to at least join them for Friday afternoon drinks, but she said she couldn't." He frowned. "It always seemed like she really wanted to go, but …"

He appeared to be trying to remember something.

"What is it?" I asked.

"I don't know. Probably nothing. It's just … our company is very big on team bonding and they put on a few little events a year. Nothing too major. More like social things. Like a few months ago they decided to do their own version of the Amazing Race."

"Like the reality show?" I asked, remembering the show where teams raced against each other in a sort of treasure hunt.

"Yeah, like that. Anyway, our manager, Kim, wanted Callie to join in, but Phillip told her he wanted Callie to stay back so she could finish a project she was supposed to be working on. Maybe it's nothing, but sometimes it felt like he really had it in for her. He was always making her stay late on stuff that she didn't need to stay late for."

I recalled my conversation with Miranda earlier that day and wondered if Callie's reluctance to join her workmates for drinks had something to do with what she had been hinting. I didn't want to voice my suspicions in case I was wrong, but I had the horrible feeling that it had everything to do with what had happened to her.

I decided to move the conversation away from Callie and we began to talk about music we liked. Tom seemed to like heavy rock, like Led Zeppelin, which I thought was all right, but certainly nothing I could tolerate for very long. We began debating the merits of various songs and bands, ending up in a mock argument. A short while later a couple of friends of his came in and weighed in on the debate.

Despite having never really been much of a fan of nightclubs, I was enjoying myself. One of Tom's friends asked me to dance to a reasonably slow song. I'm no dancer and my sense of rhythm is hopeless, but he didn't seem to mind, holding me close, but not too close.

As we danced, I could see Tom watching us with a strange look on his face. When he got up and approached us, I realised what it was. It was the same look he had given Jake the night of the basketball game. He was jealous.

His friend looked at him for a few tense seconds, then nodded and pulled away so Tom could dance with me. He gathered me in his arms, holding me in such a way that it seemed to be a message to his friends that I was definitely hands off.

I was even more surprised as the song came to an end when he cupped my cheek with one hand, his thumb stroking gently, then his lips closed over mine. As he kissed me, I felt lightheaded. I stared up at him as he pulled away, not sure what to do. Did I kiss him back? Should I walk away?

I knew what my body wanted, but the question was, were we ready for such intimacy?

Tom was quiet as he drove home. I wondered what he was thinking, what he was feeling. Whether he thought kissing me was a mistake. All I knew was that one kiss was never going to be enough. I could never be happy with one. I wanted more.

He pulled up in the driveway and turned off the ignition. My hand was on the door handle, ready to open the latch, when he touched my shoulder.

"Janet, about before ..."

"Tommy, you don't have to explain," I said. "I got it."

"Do you? I just ... when I saw Smitty dancing with you, the way you were dancing, I couldn't ..."

"You were jealous," I finished.

He nodded, looking upset, or possibly guilty. I couldn't tell which. "I don't know why I ... they were telling me they thought you were cute and I just felt I didn't want anyone looking at you that way." He bit his lip. "Anyone but me, I guess. Does that make me a bad person?"

"No," I said. "I'm glad you told me."

"I don't know where to go from here, Janet."

"Tommy, there's no reason why we have to rush into anything," I said. "I mean, I know I want to explore whatever this is, but I'm not going to just jump into bed with you either. I'm not built like that."

"Neither am I," he admitted. "Don't get me wrong. I've had one-night stands when I was a lot younger, but I'm thirty-eight years old, Janet. I don't want to have sex with someone just for the sake of it."

"Me either," I told him. "I like what we're building here. Besides, there are no hard and fast rules to this.

We don't have to follow along with everyone else's idea of what a relationship should be."

He looked down at his lap for a moment and sighed softly.

"It's not just that," he said. "It's sort of what I said last night. I don't want to get into something with you only to find out that your feelings are just mixed up in your grief for Callie. She was your best friend. I get that. I mean, I don't mean to sound harsh, or … whatever."

"Tommy, if there's one thing I learned from what happened to her it's that I don't want to spend the rest of my life thinking what if. I know I said all this last night, but I do have feelings for you, and I'm not confused about what those feelings are. The thing is, when it comes to love and relationships, yes, it's a risk, but it's one I'm willing to take."

He reached over and touched a curl, winding it around his finger.

"But can you let her go?" he asked.

I frowned at him, trying to make sense of what he was saying. I guessed he thought that my inability to let go of my need to know the truth about her death was the one thing stopping us from exploring this relationship. I couldn't let her go. Not yet. I felt like there was something else she was trying to tell me through her journals. Something I was sure I was so close to.

"I can't," I said, shaking my head. "Not yet."

He turned his head and looked out the window. He didn't reply, but he didn't have to. Tom didn't want to make it a condition of our burgeoning relationship, but

I felt that was exactly what he was doing anyway. I guessed he was afraid that once I did let Callie go that I would discover my feelings weren't as real as I assured him they were.

It hurt, a little, but I understood. He wasn't willing to take that risk. We'd taken a step forward that night, in the club, but then we'd gone two steps back again. It was frustrating. I understood, but I still found it frustrating anyway.

"Please don't think I'm rejecting you," he said. "You're a beautiful woman and I really do want to explore this, but I just don't know how it can work when your mind is still so full of Callie and what happened."

"I get it," I said quietly.

He turned his head and looked at me, his gaze questioning. I bit my lip, gazing back at him, wanting to get lost in his eyes. I realised it wasn't about him not wanting to get involved with me, but more that he was afraid I would suddenly discover that these feelings weren't real.

He'd clearly been burned badly in a past relationship and it was a case of once bitten, twice shy.

"Someone really hurt you badly, didn't they?" I said softly.

He balked slightly, appearing a little unnerved by the way I had read him so well.

"There was a girl, a few years ago. We even talked about getting married, but ... I don't really know what happened. She cheated on me with a man I thought was my friend. When I confronted her about it, she told me that what we'd felt was an illusion. She wasn't trying to be cruel but she felt she had fallen for what was on the surface, and what was underneath wasn't what she wanted."

I winced in sympathy. She'd basically told Tom he was too shallow for her, basing her opinion of his character on his looks. She couldn't have been more wrong.

"Well, you're better than that," I told him. "She didn't deserve you."

"Damn straight," he said with a self-deprecating laugh.

CHAPTER TWENTY-THREE

Over the next few days, Tom and I spent a lot of time together. I was still reading Callie's journals, but I began to spend less time reading and more time just enjoying myself.

Tom had chosen to take a week off work, just so he could spend some time with me and we went out for lunch or just out walking along the shore, careful not to walk out on the mudflats. Tom had told me of coming across a man in a four-wheel drive vehicle which had got bogged down in the mudflats. The man had ended up red-faced as it became clear he knew nothing about those types of vehicles and like many others in Auckland, had only bought the vehicle as some kind of status symbol.

On Monday night, Tom decided to take me out to another basketball game — this time a minor game between two local clubs. While it was not quite as exciting as the previous week's game, I still enjoyed cheering for my chosen team. Tom had chosen to support the other team which saw us bickering back and forth.

While he had many similarities to Callie, especially in his self-deprecating sense of humour, a love of basketball was not one of them. Callie had been the least athletically-inclined person I knew. Not that she had been lazy. She just never understood why some people became obsessed with sports.

I recalled a few mock arguments between us when we'd been younger, although now I had cause to wonder if part of it might have been a little bit of resentment because I had chosen to go to a school sports event rather than spend time with her. I had never wanted her to feel left out of things in my life but despite the fact we were the best of friends I had always thought it was important that we cultivated other interests. Friends shouldn't be dependent on each other to entertain them.

I mentioned this to Tom, who assured me I hadn't done anything wrong. He, too, believed that it wasn't necessary to always share the same interests. He liked other sports, like rugby, whereas I wasn't a huge fan of it, and I liked modern dance while he screwed his nose up when I mentioned it. I liked the fact that we didn't always agree on things. It made for some healthy debate between us.

When we weren't out exploring, we stayed at Tom's place, sitting in the living room, watching movies or just talking. Tom sat in one armchair while I sat in the other. Whether he had meant to or not, Tom had put some distance between us and it felt like a line had been drawn. I understood why, even if it felt strange that we could have shared so much yet to suddenly have this illusion of distance.

Still, as we talked, I began to realise that despite the similarities he had shared with Callie, there were some subtle differences.

I liked that I could argue the merits of various things with Tom, on any subject. We could talk for hours. Callie and I had always been able to talk for a long time as well, but the things we talked about tended to be restricted to 'girl' stuff, whereas Tom was fairly knowledgeable on a number of things.

I had never been much of a reader as a child, but Tom had a collection of books he had always loved. He teased me about my lack of literary knowledge, but it was clear he didn't mind in the slightest. It seemed as far as he was concerned it was not necessarily a bad thing.

I had once gone out with a man who had thought a couple should want to do everything together. He hadn't cared what my interests were, as long as I only spent time doing what he wanted to do. It had been as if I wasn't allowed thoughts or feelings of my own. While the relationship hadn't been abusive, I hadn't liked how possessive he was becoming and left him. I'd heard that he had found a girlfriend who had made him take a good look at himself and realise just how bad his behaviour was.

When I had first learned that, I had been a little sad, as I had liked the man, and I had wondered why this girl had succeeded where I had failed. Still, I knew now that walking away from him had been the best thing for me to do. Otherwise, I thought, I would probably never have given Tom a chance.

I had decided to stay until the weekend, giving

myself the Saturday to drive back to Napier. Tom tried to convince me to stay longer, since I still had two more weeks before I had to go back to work, but there were things I wanted to do at home. I could tell that despite his ambivalent feelings about our growing feelings for each other, he did want to explore it a little more. So did I, but I had begun to think he was right to want to take it slowly. So many relationships fell apart because people were in too much of a hurry.

The Thursday before I was due to leave it was raining, so Tom curled up in his chair, reading a book. He'd offered to get a movie, but there was nothing I really wanted to watch, so we both settled for reading. I had pulled out Callie's last journal and made myself comfortable on the couch, my shoes off, feet tucked under me.

I had told Tom my suspicions about what had been going on the last few months of Callie's life, but I knew there was no way to confirm any of it without reading her diary. Tom was still a little concerned, but he had realised there was no changing my mind on this.

The journal was only half-full and the entries had been kept fairly short. Most of them had been about how Callie hated her job and problems she was having with her flatmate, who seemed not to notice that there was something going on. Callie had been trying to save money for the trip we had talked about, but Susan had been buying various things for the house and it seemed she had been bullying Callie to come up with half the money, which even Tom told me was totally unfair.

I could tell just from reading that Callie was going downhill fairly rapidly. There had been times in her journal entries when she had been fairly upbeat, clearly trying to be positive, until something else happened that would make her come crashing down again. Yet these entries were full of self-loathing, telling me there was something seriously wrong with her. She repeated herself many times, as if the same messages were being transmitted into her brain. Almost like some kind of brainwashing.

I remembered something Jake had said about the little characters on the shoulder. It felt like the little devil was constantly feeding those negative messages into Callie's mind, drowning out the positive messages from the other side until she could only hear the negative.

Something was making her very unhappy and as much as I wanted to blame Susan for it, I began getting hints that it was something else. Or something else. Despite knowing how things would end, dreading that ending, I kept reading.

I supposed if this had been some Hollywood type movie, someone would come along, like a fairy godmother, and rescue Callie from her miserable life, sweep her off somewhere and she would be healed by some miracle cure. But this was not Hollywood, and I knew help wasn't coming for her.

As much as it hurt, I still needed to read the entries, trying to find some clue.

I AM SUCH A LOSER!

I am going to quit my job. I have to. I am so close to having a nervous breakdown it isn't funny.

Why is it so hard for me to get the job I want? I tried for this other job but they wouldn't even give me an interview.

I know it's pretty tough out there right now, but I've got enough experience. I've done everything they asked for in the job ad, so why didn't they want me?

I wonder if Phil's said something. It's like he doesn't want to let me go, but I know he doesn't appreciate the things I do around here. I hate that.

You know what he said the other day? He said no one would want me anyway because I'm such a loser.

God why? Why was I born to be so unlucky?

I really hate Susan at the moment. She's got a good job and gets big money but she treats me like dirt and expects me to pay for half of everything. It's no wonder she can't keep a boyfriend. She's so demanding, it's like as soon as they find out what she's like they go running for the hills.

She's always complaining about the fact I never spend any time with her, yet she makes it so hard for me to even talk to her. The other day I wanted to watch something on tv but no ... it was her tv, even though I paid for half of it, so she got to watch what she wanted and she didn't even care. And she wonders why I don't want to spend time with her.

She complained the other day about the grocery bill, but she was the one who picked out expensive stuff. Like she bought this luxury soap which was twice the price of a normal soap. Why? Because she liked the smell of it. Who cared? There's cheap stuff that smells just as good.

Sometimes I just really hate her. She has no idea what it's like to live pay cheque to pay cheque.

I had to go back to the doctor today. I kept breaking down in tears. He just gave me a prescription for more anti-depressants. Like I really need more of those! He asked me if I was feeling suicidal. What kind of question is that?

I couldn't tell him, but I think about that a lot. I can't deal with everything going on in my life right now. Between my flatmate and my job, and everything else, I just don't know if I can take any more.

I can't talk to Janet. She's in such a good place right now. I mean, I know what they say. Being around such negativity can really drag a person down. I don't want to do that to her. I know what she said about always being there for me, but I just can't.

I don't want to admit that all our plans for going on holiday just aren't going to work. That would be like admitting failure.

I sighed. So much of Callie's stubbornness and pride came through her words and it hurt that she had been too proud to tell me she was having problems. I wished she had known that I would have dropped everything in a second to help her.

I had never thought of her problems dragging me down. While she had been negative at times, there were so many good things about her that I felt if I could have just got that through to her, I might have been able to prevent her suicide.

I remembered something from a movie where a character was telling this girl how special she really was. She had told him the bad stuff was easier to believe. In Callie's case, that was definitely true.

I glanced at Tom, who appeared to be absorbed in his own book, a thriller by his favourite author. Yet I could tell from the stiff way he was sitting that he wasn't so deep into the book that he hadn't noticed me getting upset.

He looked up at me.

"You okay?" he asked.

I tried for a weak smile. "I'm fine," I said.

He put his book down and got to his feet. "Maybe we need a cup of tea."

"I'm fine," I repeated. "Really."

He bit his lip. "I hear that you're fine, but I can tell you're upset. You've got that look in your eyes."

"What look?" I asked, frowning at him.

"The look that says you're trying to curl in upon yourself. Like you don't want to let anyone in. I notice you do that when you're reading something pretty intense."

"It's the last journal," I told him, holding up the book.

"Oh," he said, nodding in understanding. "Want to talk about it?"

"No. Not yet anyway."

"Okay. Well, I'm going to make some tea anyway. Feel like a cup?"

"Thanks," I said.

Deciding it was a good time for a break, I put the book down beside me and went to help him make the tea. He had bought a coffee cake and we sat at the breakfast bar, just talking about general things as we ate. Tom once again teased me about my sweet tooth. He was clearly trying to lighten the mood.

By the time we had finished our drinks, the rain had stopped and the sun was coming out, shining through the windows. Tom left the room to go and do something in his bedroom and I decided to sit in the sun with the journal. Tom had a wicker chair with a big cushion which sat next to the window and I sat with my legs crossed, reading.

There was more talk about suicide, but not enough for me to think she had really been contemplating it. Her moods were worrying, however, getting increasingly darker.

She began hinting at something else happening in her life and it had been making her even more unhappy. It wasn't until I began reading the next passage that I was able to put the pieces together, as if everything leading up to now had been part of some huge jigsaw puzzle and this was the last piece. All the things Miranda had said about Callie's talks with her mother, the problems at work, all added up to one thing.

I don't know what to do. I'm scared. He says he's going to tell everyone I'm some kind of … I don't want to say it. It's not true. It's not! I never wanted this in the first place. I don't even like him!

I applied for another job. I had an interview and everything but they never asked me in for a second interview and when I contacted them to find out what was happening they never replied. I keep thinking maybe he's done something to sabotage it. I didn't want to put him down as a reference. I wanted to put down the manager because I know she likes me, but they wanted the name of my direct supervisor. I really didn't want to, especially after what's been happening. Besides, I've been there longer than he has and I know more about the job than he does.

Oh god. I'm never going to be free!

Not long after that I read something which I realised

had been Callie's breaking point.

I found out today that he did sabotage me. He told them I was totally unreliable and I couldn't do my job properly. I didn't even have to ask. He was so smug as he told me he knew I'd gone for a job interview and it didn't matter because he was never going to let me go. He liked having power over me.

I tried to break it off, but he won't leave me alone. He cornered me in the break room today, made me ... there was no one else around. He knows I come in early to get some work done and it's like he's stalking me. I told him I didn't want this but he won't take no for an answer. Then he said if I told anyone he would make me sorry. Then he grabbed my arms and squeezed so hard I thought he would break them.

He said he didn't know why I even tried since no one would ever want me. That I was ugly and stupid and so many horrible things.

I know Susan saw the bruises. She doesn't know about him. I guess she thinks I'm still just a naïve little virgin. I told her the bruises were nothing. I tend to bump into stuff and I guess she believed it. I can't tell her what's really going on. If I did, I know he'll do something bad to her. He said he would hurt anyone if I tried to tell them. Even my friends at work.

I sat up, my feet on the floor, leaning forward in the chair, my eyes practically glued to the page. I was vaguely aware of Tom being in the room, although I hadn't realised he had come in until that moment. I just couldn't believe what I was reading. When she began describing in detail what he was doing to her I couldn't help the gasp of horror. She never said his name but it was easy enough for me to work it out.

My stomach churned and I felt sick, the journal dropping to the floor, making a soft thud on the hardwood flooring. I had my answer. He'd forced her into something she didn't want and the more she tried to get away, the tighter he gripped her. Callie was trapped in a nightmare and the only way she could escape was by dying.

I had known a few women in abusive relationships and I used to wonder why they stayed. Now, just reading Callie's journal, I understood. The men had power over them. They stayed because they were utterly convinced they would never be free and terrified of what their partners would do. Their abusive partners would never have willingly let them go.

What was happening between Callie and 'him' was more than a case of domestic abuse. He was someone who had authority over her and he'd used it to force her into a relationship she didn't want, forcing her to keep quiet. She had been left with no option, not even to go to police and report rape, or abuse, because he would have made it seem like she was a willing partner, telling her he would kill her if she told anyone. He'd taken advantage of his position and terrified her into silence.

I knew things had come to a head when she wrote there was no other way out. It was her last entry.

CHAPTER TWENTY-FOUR

The room was silent, so silent a pin dropping would have almost been deafening. I sat there, frozen with anger and shock. I didn't know what to think, or what to do. Part of me wanted to find the man and do to him what I imagined he had done to Callie. To leave him so paralysed with fear and loathing that he could never do to anyone else what he had done.

The sound of the front door closing pulled me out of my stupor and I looked up, realising Tom was watching me. He had a strange look on his face which made me wonder what he had seen.

Miranda came in, her backpack slung over one shoulder. She frowned as she looked from Tom to me, clearly wondering what was up.

"Uh, hey," she said.

Tom moved first, pasting on a smile.

"Hey. How was school?"

"It was okay. I got this big assignment that I …" Miranda looked at me with a puzzled expression, her words trailing off. "You okay?" she asked.

"I'm fine," I said, my voice suddenly hoarse.

"You don't look fine," she said. "You look like you're going to be sick or something."

I bit my lip. The nausea had begun to settle in my stomach but I knew if I moved it could very well upset things again. I shook my head at her.

"Really, I'm okay," I said, denying the horror I was feeling.

She shrugged, clearly not happy with my response, but knowing there was little she could do about it.

"Okay. Well, I need to get started on this before I have to go to work."

She went out, going to her bedroom to ostensibly get started on her homework. Tom looked at me.

"What's wrong?" he asked.

I sighed. "Please don't ask me."

"It's something you read in there, isn't it?"

I wanted to pick up the journal as he approached me, but I stayed frozen.

"I … I know why she did it."

"Tell me," he said softly.

"I can't," I replied, shaking my head.

"Why not?"

How could I tell him? He worked with the man and he cared about Callie. If he knew what had been done to her, there was no telling what he would do. Part of me wanted to protect him from the horrifying truth. Then there was the thought that he might be so angry he would do something he would regret.

There was no way to answer it without upsetting him.

"Janet," he said softly. "You need to talk about this."

"I can't," I said. "You have to understand. This isn't something I can easily explain away."

"Janet," he said, crouching down beside me. "I know that most of what was in Callie's journals was private. But I can see you're upset about something and holding it in isn't going to help."

"I'm sorry," I replied, looking down at him. His blue eyes were clouded with worry and it was the last thing I wanted.

I needed to get away from my thoughts. My skin felt like something was crawling all over me every time I thought about what I had read.

"Let's go out," I said finally. "Please?"

"Where do you want to go?" he asked softly.

"Anywhere, just ... I don't know."

"We could take a drive," he suggested. "Maybe out to Piha."

Piha was a beach community about three quarters of an hour's drive from Tom's house. It was known to be one of the most famous surf beaches in the country, mostly for its wildness. I think there had even been a reality programme on television following the day-to-day lives of the lifeguards as they worked.

"That sounds like a good idea," I replied.

It looked to be a fairly windy afternoon as we drove out to the beach, along winding roads. If the beach lived up to its reputation, it was the perfect representation for how I was feeling. My mind was in turmoil.

On the one hand, I wanted to tell Tom what I had learnt, but on the other, I was afraid of how he would react if I did. Tom was not normally a violent person but I knew just from the few conversations we'd had that he was the kind of person who couldn't stand to see an injustice done to someone. I knew he would see this the same way.

He was the kind of man I'd always pictured I would fall in love with, although neither of us were at that point yet.

Callie had laughed when I'd told her of the kind of man I pictured having a future with. I'd loved watching an English television series when I was little about three brothers who ran a veterinary practice. There had been a young guy who had owned a dog, or rather, the dog had owned him. He had become very upset when the dog had got sick. I had thought that anyone who felt that way about animals was a good person.

Thinking back, Callie never talked much about having boyfriends, or a future. She never had dreams of what her life would be like in ten years or more. It was an ominous thought, but I wondered if maybe she had known she would only have a short life.

I watched through the window as Tom negotiated the winding, narrow road, my mind in turmoil. I could just see the water as he drove downhill.

The surf was just as wild as I had read. Huge swells could be seen in the distance, violent waves breaking over the rocks. Being late autumn, it was too cold for swimming and I was glad to see no one was out risking their necks in the surf.

Tom parked the car along Marine Parade where we could look out over the water. It was too windy to get out and go for a walk, so we just sat there, not talking.

The silence was palpable.

He finally turned to look at me.

"Janet, what was in the journal that upset you?"

"I can't tell you," I said. "I don't want you to get upset. It was hard enough for me to read."

"Why would I get upset?" he asked, frowning at me.

"Trust me, you would," I assured him.

I gazed at him. He was a good man with a compassionate heart.

A few days earlier we'd been watching a television movie. It was one that had been on a long time ago, about a young woman who had been beaten and crippled by her abusive husband. They'd rescreened it for some unknown reason. Tom had been so upset he had switched it off before the movie ended. We'd talked for a long time about what he was feeling.

"I just can't stand to see someone ... a guy who's supposed to love her ... do something like that."

"It's got nothing to do with love," I told him quietly. "It's about power. Some guys think that their masculinity is in power over women."

"That's such bull," he said.

I had a theory that some men became violent because they felt threatened, like a dog guarding its territory. Most of these men were misogynistic and sexist, thinking women should be kept in their place. Still, it was only a theory.

I put my hand on his chest. I could feel his heart pounding beneath my hand.

"I know you're upset, and I know you're angry, but see, that's what makes you different from guys like that. You are a good, kind man."

He looked at me for a long moment, then smiled.

"You have a lot of faith in me, Janet."

"You have helped me get through some pretty tough moments the last few weeks. How could I not have faith in you?"

Thinking back to that moment I knew he would get very upset, I thought, if he knew everything.

I glanced at him, thinking carefully about what to say.

"You know, I've spent all this time thinking it was my fault. That I wasn't such a good friend, and that was why she did it."

"Janet, that's not true. I happen to know you were a very good friend."

I nodded, giving him a small smile. We'd talked about it before and I knew I was repeating myself, but this was something I needed to get out.

"I know. All along, in her journal, when things started coming to a head, Callie kept saying how she wanted to tell me but she was afraid. I thought she was afraid that I might react badly, tell her she was stupid. I thought she didn't have enough faith in me."

"Is that really what she thought?"

"No," I said, shaking my head.

"So it was something else?" he asked.

I couldn't tell him any more. Not if I didn't want him to put the pieces together.

"Just know that it wasn't my fault and it wasn't your fault," I told him quietly.

I saw he wasn't satisfied with that explanation but there wasn't much more I could say without telling him everything.

We sat in silence for a little while, watching the waves. Despite the wildness in the ocean, I found it calming. Maori have a deep affinity with the sea. Legend passed down from those who settled in New Zealand centuries ago has it that our ancestors came here in great canoes from Hawaiiki, our ancestral homeland. There are other legends too, but I often thought of that one when I spent time at the beach. It was one of the things I loved about the city I lived in, since it was so close to the sea.

It was also one of the things that Callie loved about it too. She would sit out on the beach for hours just watching the waves. It was a contradiction that something so wild and untamed could calm her when she was feeling at her worst but I now understood. It was like the sea was something that couldn't be controlled and contained. It couldn't be pigeonholed.

I realised that all her life, Callie had been just the opposite. She had been told who she should be, how she should feel, how she should behave. Her spirit was one that wanted to be free, but never allowed to be.

People had had power over her and in many ways, I thought her illness was her mind's way of fighting those constraints. There had been other factors of course; her self-confidence, or lack thereof, one of them, but all of it had chipped away at her until there was nothing left. I was definitely no expert on depression, and I doubted it was the same for most people, but to me it just felt like it was something Callie had experienced.

I didn't know how to explain it to Tom when I couldn't really describe it in my own head. All I could see was that many things had contributed to what had happened to Callie, but being 'imprisoned' by the man who had abused her had been the catalyst.

I finally understood what she had been trying to tell me by making sure I alone was given those journals. I was the one person who had tried to encourage her to choose her own path in life, but the need to please everyone had been too strong.

In the end, taking her own life was the only choice she could have made freely, without influence from anyone else. As much as it hurt, I knew now she was truly free. At peace.

Tom and I returned to his house, having stopped on the way for some fish and chips. The shop he ordered them from served them in what I thought was the traditional way. Battered fish and crispy, golden and thick deep-fried chips, all wrapped up in newsprint paper. Too many stores nowadays had moved away from that which I felt was a shame.

It was one of the many things that began as a tradition in England and found its way here. When I was a teenager, we didn't get a lot of takeaways, but fish'n'chips was a special treat. Often Callie would come to dinner with us and in summer we would take our meal to the beach.

I smiled as I remembered one early evening when we'd gone to sit out on the beach with the treat wrapped in newsprint. It wasn't long before the seagulls surrounded us, eager for some of our food. Callie ended up chasing them up and down the beach, annoyed at their brazenness.

Tom looked at me across the table, a half-eaten chip

in his hand.

"What are you thinking about?" he asked.

"Just nights like this, when Callie and I would take fish'n'chips to the beach and spend half our time chasing away the seagulls."

"That sounds like a nice memory," he said.

"It is."

He smiled back. "It's nice to see you smiling. You're beautiful when you smile."

I felt myself blushing and I ducked my head. He laughed and smacked me lightly on the shoulder. I grinned and shoved him back playfully, then mock glared at him as he picked up the bottle of tomato sauce and pretended to threaten me with it.

"Don't you dare!" I exclaimed, picking up the bottle of sweet chilli sauce, which he seemed to prefer. I'd teased him about his weird tastes, as much as he teased me about my sweet tooth.

He laughed again and put the sauce down. The earlier tension was forgotten as we began to bicker good-naturedly, teasing each other.

It was late when we both went to bed that night, having sat up to watch some old movie from the eighties. The humour was puerile and more aimed at teenage boys than women, especially with the constant burping and sex jokes, but I got a kick out of watching Tom, who had clearly enjoyed it. He'd made popcorn and we'd ended up throwing it at each other.

For the first time since Callie died, I felt like a huge burden had been lifted.

I still had dreams, especially about Callie, but this time, the dreams were peaceful. Callie was happy.

I had one dream in which we were talking over Skype. It was hard to tell if it was really just a dream or a memory, since I didn't recall having had such a conversation, but she was telling me about a friend at work.

"He's a really sweet guy," she said. "I think you'd like him a lot."

"If you like him that much, why don't you go out with him?" I asked.

"Well, he's kind of shy, and you know how reserved I can be. Sometimes I think people can have too much in common, you know?"

I frowned at her. "What do you mean?"

"Well, it's like that thing about opposites attracting. I mean, you're really outgoing, and he's kind of reserved but that's not a bad thing."

I did get what she meant, and I realised as the dream conversation went on that she was talking about Tom. It was as if she was telling me she was giving her blessing.

CHAPTER TWENTY-FIVE

I woke up feeling refreshed and better than I had since Callie died. I practically jumped out of bed, ready to tell Tom what I had discovered.

Miranda was in the kitchen, clearly having gone for a run. She smiled at me.

"You look happy," she said.

"I am," I replied.

"I'm glad," she answered. "It's nice to see you smiling," she said, in what seemed like a repeat of Tom's words the evening before. "You're so pretty when you smile."

She put her empty bowl in the sink and began to walk past me.

"I'm gonna go take a shower," she said.

"Is Tom up?"

She frowned. "Yeah. He practically rushed out the door as I came in, said he had something to do. He looked like, well, my mum used to say that sometimes it was like she had a bee in her bonnet. I'm not sure what it was supposed to mean, but I guess she meant there was something bugging her."

"But you don't know what it was?" I asked, figuring out what she meant in her roundabout way of talking.

She shrugged. "I guess he'll tell you."

I watched as she went out, wondering what had upset Tom that he would go rushing off like that. I stepped into the kitchen to grab a cup and make myself a coffee when I happened to glance in the living room. I remembered dropping the journal on the floor after reading the final entry but I couldn't remember picking it up.

It wasn't on the floor, or on the table. I quickly looked around but it was nowhere in sight.

Had I taken it to my room? I tried to remember what I had done with it, but all I could remember was the thud as it landed on the floor.

What if Tom had read the entry and put two and two together, I thought?

I ran back to my room and quickly changed my clothes, grabbing my bag and my car keys. As I stepped outside, Tom's car was not in the driveway.

I got in my own car and backed down the driveway, narrowly missing a car which had been coming the other way. The driver beeped at me, the horn blasting loudly in the cool morning air.

The main road leading to the highway was already busy with drivers on their way to work, and I knew the motorway into the city centre would be just as busy, but I had no choice. I hoped that if Tom had only left a few minutes before then he would likely be caught up in the same traffic jam that I was. If I was lucky, maybe I could get there in time to stop him doing what I dreaded he was going to do.

It seemed I wasn't the only one who had to be somewhere in a hurry that morning. It felt like I was one of at least about ten thousand people with the same need. As the cars crawled along the motorway I heard more than a few beeps from impatient motorists, wanting to get through. There were a few near misses as cars cut across lanes of traffic to take up gaps.

This is why I hate Auckland, I thought. I could never tolerate such a commute every day. Why is it, I said to myself, sighing, that every time I'm in a hurry to be somewhere everything works against me?

I grew increasingly worried and even more impatient as the traffic continued to crawl. I had no idea how long it had been since Tom had left and I didn't dare call him on his cellphone, not wanting to get caught using my phone, even in the slow traffic. One moment of inattention and I could plough into the car in front of me. I had already seen a couple of near misses on the way.

Finally, the traffic began to speed up a little as a few drivers turned off the motorway, either on their way to work in other suburbs or too impatient to continue on at such a slow speed, intending to take the longer way into town.

It was at least forty-five minutes since I'd left the house when I turned in to the car park at Tom's office. I got out of the car, looking around for Tom's Mondeo, but it didn't appear to be around. I still had a feeling he was here and ran in, panting a little as I approached the reception desk. Melissa recognised me from the week before and smiled uncertainly at me.

"Janet?"

"Has Tom come in?" I asked breathlessly.

"Uh, yeah, he shot past me about five minutes ago. What's going on?"

"I can't go into detail, but I think he found out something which I'm guessing upset him."

"Like what?" she asked.

"I need to get up there," I said, not wanting to answer the question. I nodded my head, indicating the upper level of the office where his desk was located.

"Janet," she began.

"Melissa, I can't explain. We just need to get in there before he does something he'll regret."

She still looked dubious but I didn't want to make her angry by pushing past her and trying to bypass the security, so I just looked at her, trying to convey just how serious this could be. She bit her lip, then nodded, using her card to unlock the door.

We ran upstairs and down toward Tom's division. As we reached about halfway across the building it was fairly obvious something was going on. Half the people on the floor were crowding around a desk at the far end and I could hear shouting. Melissa looked at me and we began running.

As we got closer, I could recognise Tom's voice. He was practically screaming at another man, who cowered in the corner. A part of me was glad to see him so afraid of Tom, who was red-faced and clearly very angry.

"You sick son of a ... how could you do that to her?"

Some of the staff, especially the woman who had replaced Callie, were staring wide-eyed and fearful from their own pods, wondering what had made Tom so angry.

"Tom," Kim was saying, clearly trying to defuse the situation. She was standing beside him, pulling on his arm. "You need to calm down."

I saw with alarm and concern that Tom was waving a book around. The hard cover was red, exactly the same colour as Callie's journals. He held it aloft, as if he was about to use it to strike Philip across the face.

"Tommy!" I called.

He quickly turned his head and looked at me, then looked down.

"Janet," he said. I could hear the underlying despair in his tone, even as his voice was still filled with rage.

"Tommy, please, don't do this," I begged as I approached him cautiously, not knowing what he could do in the mood he was in. "He's not worth it."

"Yeah, Tom, don't be stupid," Phillip piped up, clearly too arrogant to realise just how stupid he was by even speaking up.

Tom turned back to him, his face screwed up with anger. Kim looked at me, then at Melissa. I could tell she wanted to call security, but that was probably the worst thing she could do.

"Kim, get him away from Tom," I said quietly.

She again looked at me with a slight frown. I nodded.

"It'll be okay," I said. "I'll talk to him."

None of the other staff members had even stepped up, although in all honesty I couldn't really blame them. It was a safe bet none of them had ever seen Tom that angry. It was another thing he had had in common with Callie. She had never been the kind of person who would get angry on her own behalf, but she would if she was standing up for someone else.

I touched Tom's arm as Kim gestured for Philip to move. He edged slowly past Tom, a wary eye on him. I didn't fail to catch the smirk on his face as soon as he began walking with Kim down to her office.

"Tommy," I said.

He didn't respond, just wrapped his arms around me and held me, his head on my shoulder. I felt the grief in his tension even as his anger slowly ebbed away.

"Come on," I coaxed gently. "Let's go down to the café and just talk."

I felt him nod his head against my shoulder. He lifted his head and heaved a deep sigh. I took his hand and began walking with him downstairs, nodding and smiling at Melissa, who looked relieved that I had managed to defuse a difficult situation.

Later I would think about why Tom had responded to me and no one else, but at that moment, all I could focus on was calming his anger.

I realised he was no longer holding the book. It must have dropped on the floor, I thought. Torn between protecting Callie's memory from her colleagues and getting Tom away from the scene, I wasn't sure what to do. Thankfully, Melissa must have noticed it as she picked it up.

"Janet, I think Tom dropped this," she said quietly.

I nodded. "Thanks Melissa," I said, taking it and holding it tightly in one hand.

She walked ahead of us, shaking her head at the other workers who had been watching but hadn't lifted a finger to help. Typical, I snorted to myself. It was little wonder Callie hadn't been able to trust anyone with what was happening, if all they ever did was stand by and watch but do little else.

I supposed I could understand it, since it was the typical reaction of a large percentage of the population. I'd heard of it happening before where people would stand by and watch rather than step in. I think in the end that was one of the things that hurt Callie the most. She couldn't stand by and watch but it was patently obvious that the world had become too apathetic, too self-centred to even care.

Melissa glanced at me with a small smile and I knew she was thinking the same thing. God knew what she would think if she knew the truth about Callie's death. I imagined if she did, there would be a very strongly worded email circulating around the building.

We managed to get downstairs without anyone trying to stop us. I assumed they had all heard how angry Tom was and decided it would be more prudent to give us a wide berth. I wasn't in the mood to explain to anyone what was really going on. Melissa made us sit on the couch while she got the barista to make us both coffees. With a smile, she left us, saying she had to take care of reception.

I turned to look at Tom. He appeared calmer, although he was still gripping my hand like it was a lifeline.

"I know you're angry," I said.

"I know why you didn't want to tell me," he replied. "But I still wish you had."

"I thought you would be upset if you knew."

"Yeah, you said that. You should have told me," he

admonished me.

In hindsight, the fact that I was proved right didn't negate the fact that I probably should have told him anyway. I might have been able to prevent him going off half-cocked the way he had, I told myself.

"Please don't," I said. "Don't be mad."

"I am, but not at you. I still … if you had talked to me, we might have been able to talk this out," he said, confirming what I was thinking.

"I know," I said, "and that was my mistake. I'm sorry. I thought I was doing the right thing in not telling you. You loved her too."

He ran a hand over his hair, scratching at the back of his head and mussing up his hair.

"I did love her. As a friend, Janet. Callie and I had a lot in common."

I frowned at the 'friend' comment even though I was secretly happy that he had felt the need to add it.

The barista came over with our coffees but didn't make a comment at the way we both looked. I imagined it looked pretty bad.

"I just wish she had come to me and told me she was in trouble."

"This is not your fault, Tom. She talked about you in the journal. She said you were always supportive and she thought of you as a good friend. You listened to her when she needed it the most."

"It wasn't enough," he said with a sigh.

"Tommy, don't. Please don't start thinking you didn't do enough for her. It's like me thinking this was my fault. If it's anyone's fault, it's his," I added, glancing up in the direction of the offices upstairs. "He made her afraid to tell anyone."

I grabbed some sugar packets from the table in front of us and sweetened my coffee, then sipped it. It was bitter, but I wasn't going to complain. Tom grimaced as he tasted his own coffee.

"Ugh, this is bitter," he said, reaching for a couple of packets of sugar.

It was one more thing we had in common.

I waited until he had settled back with his coffee before I turned to look at him. We were silent for a few moments, just gazing at each other. It was as if we could tell each other everything we were feeling without even having to utter a word.

"Tom, as hard as it's been trying to understand what happened and why it happened, I finally realised something last night. Maybe it sounds a little weird, but Callie was the kind of person who was never meant to be caged. She spent far too much time trying to please everyone but in the end it just hurt her more."

"So you're saying he tried to cage her."

"It wasn't just him, but I guess what he did to her was just the proverbial straw. I mean, her dad tried to make her be something she wasn't, even though I don't think he really understood what he was doing to her. She hid her illness because she was afraid people would think the worst of her if she told them. And then he comes along and he forces her into something she doesn't want and when she tries to get away from it ..."

"He threatens her," Tom finished. "He said she was weak."

"She wasn't weak," I told him. "Vulnerable, but not

weak. Look at the way she took Miranda under her wing. The thing is, that was Callie. She found it so easy to stand up for others, but she couldn't do it for herself because she was too busy trying to live up to everyone else's expectations. They just didn't know any better."

I became aware of someone approaching us and looked up. Kim looked upset.

"I've just been talking to Philip. He admitted he and Callie had some kind of relationship." She sighed and shook her head, telling us of his arrogant attitude. He was smug, clearly not thinking he did anything wrong. "It's like he doesn't even care that she died. I just don't understand him. How can you just be that uncaring about someone you were in a relationship with?"

I didn't think Kim was naïve, but clearly she had not really understood the kind of person Philip was. Not for the first time, I thought that if only Callie had gone to her, she would have done something. Kim obviously cared a great deal about her co-workers and she would be devastated if she knew the full truth.

"Relationship. Yeah, if you'd like to call it that," Tom said with a snort. Kim frowned at him, then looked at me for an explanation. I knew she would never be able to let this go.

"What else did he say?" I asked.

"He claimed Tom attacked him because he was jealous. He knew Callie and Tom were friends, but tried to make out it was more than that."

"It wasn't, and I wasn't jealous," Tom said. "I was angry at the way he treated her."

Kim frowned again. While I was unsure about

telling her, I had begun to see that Tom was right. By not talking about it with him, he'd had time to stew over things and had reacted badly to what he'd read.

"Callie talked about it in her diary," I explained. "He used his position of authority over her to take advantage, forced her into the relationship, continually undermined her self-esteem until she had virtually nothing left. He abused her, emotionally and I believe physically as well. Callie mentioned bruises in the journal."

"God," Kim said. "Like I said the other day, I knew something was going on, but I didn't know it was this. Poor Callie. I wish she'd told me."

"She was afraid, Kim," I said quietly. "He told her he would hurt her or her friends if she told anyone, and she believed him. Even when she tried to get away, get another job, he lied about her references."

"She didn't deserve this."

"No one does," Tom said, his voice rising. I squeezed his hand and looked at him, and he subsided.

"I'm going to call the company CEO. At the very least, there should be disciplinary action, but I'm thinking we should bring the police into this," Kim said.

"Sure, and they'll do what, exactly?" Tom asked bitterly.

"Tommy, that's not helping," I said.

"Makes me feel better," he replied and I saw a small smile.

I knew this would take gentle handling. I squeezed his hand, reminding him that he wasn't alone in this.

"Tommy, getting angry over this and threatening a

guy like Philip won't bring Callie back, but there are other things we can do."

Kim nodded. "Janet's right, Tom. And we'll talk about this on Monday when you're back at work."

"What about Phil?" he asked.

"I've sent him home and told him not to come back until I've talked to the CEO." Kim looked at me uncertainly. "Is that Callie's diary?" she asked, indicating the book I'd placed on the couch beside me.

"Yeah," I said warily, trying to avoid the temptation to place a protective hand over it. I wasn't sure if Callie would have wanted Kim to know.

"Can I have it? I may need it for evidence."

I bit my lip. On the one hand, Kim was right. If they were going to take action against Philip, they needed to be able to back themselves up with evidence. What he'd done to Callie was wrong, although it was hard to say whether his actions were actually criminal. Still, I wasn't sure Callie would want this getting out.

"He has to answer for what he's done," Kim said gently. "Callie was a good person and she didn't deserve this," she repeated. Again I was struck with how much respect I heard in her voice for Callie. Maybe there had been one or two people in the office who hadn't liked Callie, but I wondered if that was because they didn't really know her and didn't take the time to get to know her. Everyone else gave me the impression they really liked her.

"Okay," I said, giving her the book.

"Thank you, Janet," she said. "I promise I'll get this back to you."

I nodded, my eyes filling with tears. Tom patted my

leg and I glanced at him. He was clearly still upset but now we were supporting each other.

CHAPTER TWENTY-SIX

By the time we made it back to Tom's place, it was close to noon. I busied myself making something to eat in Tom's kitchen since neither of us had had any breakfast.

Tom confessed he had spent half the night wondering what had upset me, even though I'd seemed to perk up after dinner. It had bothered him that after everything else we'd shared this was one thing I couldn't share with him.

After we'd eaten, I could see he was tired and still upset over the revelations. I tried to coax him into going back to bed for a while, although I knew it wouldn't take much coaxing. He had dark circles under his eyes.

He took my hand and pulled me with him.

"You really should get some sleep," I told him as he pulled me down on the bed with him.

"I don't want to be alone," he said. "Stay with me."

I wanted to, but I wasn't sure it would help the situation. He shook his head, telling me that it really wasn't anything more than him needing to be close to me.

"Janet. Talk to me."

Giving in, although if I had to admit it, it hadn't really been that much of a struggle, I lay down with him. We both lay on our sides, facing each other, hands touching.

He wanted to know how I could be so calm after learning something so upsetting.

"It's like I said. I realised a few things about Callie. Something I had never really understood before. You were right, you know. I should have let her go."

He shook his head. "I know you, Janet. You would never have been able to come to terms with it if you hadn't learned the truth. As bad as it is."

I nodded in agreement. He was right. Now that I knew the truth, knew and understood everything, I could let her go. As horrible as her death was, I could be happy knowing that she was finally free of the burdens she'd felt most of her life.

I knew it wasn't going to be easy. Callie had been my best friend for nearly twenty-eight years and we'd shared so much. I knew there would be times when I would still get upset, still get angry over what had happened to her, but I couldn't be angry at her. She was finally free and that was all she had ever wanted.

I could think of her with love.

"I had a dream about her last night," I said. "We were talking. About you, actually. Although she never actually said it was you. I just knew."

Tom frowned at me. "About me?"

"I can't remember if we ever talked about you before, but in the dream, it felt like she knew we'd be good for each other."

He smiled. "That sounds like her. She mentioned you a few times in our conversations, told me what a great friend you were. That's why I found it so hard to understand you blaming yourself for what happened."

I nodded. I understood that now.

"I guess what I found hard was that she never wanted to talk about her depression. Callie had real self-esteem issues. She never considered herself to be anyone special, but ..."

"She <u>was</u> special," Tom confirmed.

"She'd been put down most of her life," I explained. "It was hard for her to take compliments."

I knew a couple of people who had felt the same way. While I was studying at Otago, I had supported myself with a part-time job at a bar and there had been a girl who was also a student. I had once found her crying in the toilets in the bar and had asked her what was wrong.

It turned out she had the same illness as Callie, although I hadn't known about Callie then. She was going through major stress with her studies, working almost full-time hours and having problems with her parents.

The difference between her and my best friend, however, was that she wasn't afraid to talk about it. She didn't believe something like depression should be kept behind closed doors. She didn't care if her co-workers knew about it, having decided that it was better them knowing about her illness than trying to hide it when the stress got the better of her.

She was now a psychiatrist in Sydney and happily

married with two kids. She also spent a lot of time working with people with similar illnesses.

"I guess we all get a distorted view of ourselves," Tom admitted. "I mean, I've always been told I'm good-looking, but I just see an ordinary guy when I look in the mirror."

I shrugged. I often felt the same way, although I had never gone as far as calling myself unattractive. I've always been modest about my looks. I supposed I looked as good as any other woman.

When I tried to explain this to Tom, he shook his head.

"You are beautiful, Janet. Don't ever forget that."

"So are you. It's not your looks either, although granted, you are pretty hot ..."

"Oh, I know."

I punched his shoulder playfully.

"Get the ego on you," I said and he laughed. I went on. "What I was trying to say, before you so rudely interrupted me ..."

He raised an eyebrow in a mocking expression. I punched him again.

"You are a very bad man, Mr McFadden."

"Who me? I'm a perfect angel."

"Yeah, right!" I replied.

He laughed again. I loved to hear him laugh.

We continued talking, sharing confidences. He told me things about his childhood that he'd never told anyone else. I began telling him about the various things Callie and I had done when we were children, able to relate the stories without the little ache which had accompanied them up until now.

I knew with an absolute certainty that I really was ready to let her go.

Tom and I slept together in his bed that night. There was no sex, but neither of us were ready for that. We had spent most of that day just talking, helping each other come to terms with the things we'd learned in just those few hours.

The next day, Saturday, I was packing my things, ready to drive back home to Napier. I was torn. Part of me wanted to stay with Tom and the other part was missing my little house.

Tom came in as I was struggling with my suitcase. I had been lazy and hadn't folded my clothes, just stuffed them in. Tom gently pushed me away and zipped it up.

"I wish you'd stay," he said, sighing.

"I can't." Not yet, anyway, I thought.

He bit his lip, then gestured with his thumb down the hall to the living room.

"Uh, I just got a phone call from Marcus. You know the company CEO. He spoke with Kim about what happened and he's contacted the police. He doesn't know if they'll decide to press charges against Phil, but at least the police are going to investigate. Marcus is going to talk to an employment lawyer but either way, Phil is out of there. He won't be welcome back."

I doubted whether anything would come of the police investigation but it sounded like Tom's company was taking the matter very seriously. Callie would still get justice, I thought.

I started to pick up the suitcase and Tom stopped me with a hand on my arm.

"Stay," he said.

"I can't," I repeated.

He put his arms around me and kissed me softly. We'd talked the night before, basically declaring our intentions. We were finally on the same page where our relationship was going, ready to take that leap.

I had been asking myself the question over and over. Did I see a future with him? At that point, I wasn't sure, but I was more than willing to find out.

Tom picked up the suitcase and carried it out to my car. I paused in the living room. Miranda was watching a DVD, but paused it and stood up, hugging me.

"I'm really glad you came," she said.

We'd told her everything. Miranda had, of course, been upset when she had learned why Callie had done it, but Tom and I had agreed that she should know. Given the police investigation and the coroner's hearing in a few months, which was required in a case like this, she would probably have learned the truth anyway.

She canted her head and looked at me.

"You are going to, you know ..."

I wasn't sure what she was wanting to say, but I had a feeling she was meaning more than keeping in touch. She was clearly all for Tom and I exploring our feelings further, although what direction that would take was undecided.

"Don't worry," I said. "I'll be calling so often you'll get sick of me."

She shook her head. "Not a chance," she laughed.

Tom had quietly confessed to me that before he'd asked Miranda to come and live with him he had worried about her. After everything that had happened in her short life — all she had lost, he was concerned it might all be too much for the teenager. I had a feeling Miranda was strong enough to handle it. Besides, I'd assured him, she had us now.

Tom came back in, followed by Jake, who must have known I was leaving today.

"Hey," he said. "Heading back?"

I nodded. "Yeah."

He glanced at Miranda, who smiled and went back to watching her DVD, her feet curled up under her on the couch. Tom gestured toward the kitchen and we sat at the breakfast bar. Tom set about making coffee. Jake sat beside me.

"So how are you doing?" he asked.

"I'm okay." He looked at me with a dubious expression, so I smiled. "Really, I'm okay. It's getting better."

"Well, call me an interfering ass or whatever, but what I said before goes. If you need someone impartial to talk to, give me a call any time." He placed a business card on the bench and slid it over toward me.

I couldn't help thinking how completely wrong I had been about Jake when I'd first met him. Maybe first impressions counted for a lot of things, but they weren't always right.

"Thanks," I said. "I appreciate that."

Tom handed me a cup of my favourite coffee with a slight smirk. I remembered the awful coffee we'd had the day before and smiled back at him. Maybe it wasn't the greatest of moments, but it was still a moment we'd shared. One of many we would share in the future, I hoped.

Jake left shortly afterwards, wishing me a safe drive home. Tom and I lingered over the coffee. I wanted time to slow down, find some way of delaying the moment we would have to say goodbye. As I glanced at the clock, I sighed. I couldn't delay it any longer.

Tom walked me out to my car, wrapping his arms around me. He kissed me. It didn't feel like a kiss goodbye. There was so much promise in that kiss, as if it could say what neither of us could say out loud.

"Call me when you get home, okay?" he said.

"I promise," I told him.

He pulled away, but continued to hold my hand, his thumb stroking the blade. I could see he was torn, his expression full of anguish.

I leaned forward and gave him a brief kiss, then pulled away and got in my car. He watched from the driveway as I reversed onto the road, then followed as I put the car in drive, watching from the footpath as I began to drive down the street.

I had managed to hold back the tears in front of him, but as I drove away they fell unbidden.

I knew then that I'd found something amazing. Through all the pain of losing my best friend, I had found something that had given me hope.

EPILOGUE

Almost One Year Later

A light breeze was blowing, whipping at my skirt and causing a loose tendril of hair to fall across my face. Autumn was not the best time to be on the beach, even on the east coast. The weather tended to be unpredictable as the season slowly transitioned into winter.

But there was no better time to do what we had come to do. It was one year to the day that we had lost a friend, a daughter, a surrogate sister.

A hand clutched mine and I looked up with a smile at my handsome husband. Tom smiled down at me, reaching out to brush my hair back.

"You ready for this, sweetheart?" he asked.

I nodded. Tommy and I had got married a little over four months earlier. It was a quiet wedding, with my family and his. Jake was his best man and Miranda had been my bridesmaid. We both thought of Callie but it had felt like her spirit had been with us, watching over us, giving us her blessing.

Marion and Richard had also come to the wedding, as had Tom's former manager, Kim, who had wished us both luck as we started on our life's journey together.

The past few months hadn't been easy for either of us. There had been nights where I hadn't been able to sleep for thinking of Callie, and I'd called Tom, waking him up, desperate for someone to talk to.

He had never complained, never told me I was a nuisance for calling him.

We'd shared so much in those conversations, and in the weekends we'd spent together since Callie's death.

After four months of going back and forth, Tom had met my parents who were both happy that I had finally found someone I could settle down with. Dad often joked with Tommy that he had thought I was planning on being single the rest of my life to which Tommy had responded by telling Dad his parents thought the same thing.

Marion and Richard had been a little less certain of our relationship, thinking we were maybe moving a little too fast, but as I told them, I wasn't some naïve teenager who didn't know real love when I saw it. I had a great example in my mother and stepfather, and in my father, who had finally married his own, as he called it, lady friend.

Having a long-distance relationship had been hard, but figuring out the logistics of where we were going to live when we decided to get married was even worse, causing an argument that almost broke us up, until first Jake, then Grandad stepped in and made us see sense, telling us that if we really loved each other, we needed to find a compromise.

In the end, it was probably the easiest decision we had to make. I put my little house on the market and moved in with Tom about a month before we got married. Maybe I would never love Auckland, but there was at least a part of it that I did love.

We decided to start our own business together. Tom had always wanted to open a gym and he had seen other gyms with physiotherapy clinics attached to them. Miranda had decided she wanted to study to be a personal trainer and now worked part-time at the gym instead of at the restaurant. She was growing into a beautiful young woman who was working hard to succeed in life and we had no doubt she would.

Tom squeezed my hand and I looked around to watch Callie's parents walk along the beach, holding a small package. Marion smiled shyly at me, then back up at her husband. The past year had been difficult for them, but they had worked through it and come out with a stronger marriage.

There had been times when Richard had questioned his own behaviour towards his daughter and I could understand why. Even though he knew the real reason Callie had died, it still hurt him to think that he could have contributed to it.

As for the man who had hurt her, the police hadn't charged him for Callie, but a month or so after he had been fired from his job, we learned he had been arrested for assault on another woman. Given his propensity for violence, he was sent to jail.

The company Tommy had worked for had put in place stricter policies against harassment and bullying and the board had started a trust to help those who needed it get counselling. It had become a much more supportive environment and thanks to their efforts, at least two people had been able to get the help and support they needed.

"It's time," Marion said softly, handing me the package.

We'd agreed that this was something I should do, rather than Callie's parents, although they still wanted to stay. I had loved her as a sister and I knew she had loved me.

I walked to the edge, where the sand was wet from the tide, shivering a little as the cold water lapped at my bare feet. I opened the package, taking out the box and handed the paper to Tommy, who kept a supportive arm around my waist.

I closed my eyes for a moment and turned my face toward the sun, feeling its warmth. I tuned out everything but the sound of the waves, remembering that sense of peace I always felt. Tommy and I would often walk along the beach at home. The beach wasn't the same, but the feelings remained.

I opened the box and slowly poured the ashes out so they drifted in the breeze, landing on the water. I watched as what remained of my friend was taken out to sea.

Tom held me close, wrapping his arms around my waist, gently caressing my belly. We hadn't told anyone yet, as it was still early, but we knew we'd have to soon. There was just the tiny hint of a bump there.

"You know, some people believe that those we love, when they die, they come back to us." He continued stroking my belly. "Maybe this is Callie."

I didn't know if I believed in reincarnation. It wasn't something that had ever been talked about among the family. We did believe that a loved one's spirit eventually left to find its way to the traditional homeland, but Callie wasn't Maori.

I turned my head and kissed him.

"That's a beautiful thought," I said.

He smiled and kissed my nose, holding me close as we stood and watched the waves crash on the shore.

ABOUT THE AUTHOR

E M Richmond was born in the Manawatu and has been writing from the age of thirteen.

She has had her own personal health issues, including mental illness, which was the inspiration for this story.

She currently lives in Hamilton, New Zealand.